LETHAL RESUSCITATION

A DR CATHY MORELAND MYSTERY #BOOK SIX

MAIRI CHONG

ALSO BY MAIRI CHONG

For W – if I had to choose, it would be you.

1

The man groaned and turned his face to the wall.

'Scene assessment!' sang out a voice. 'It is safe to approach the victim. There are no apparent hazards.' There was a stifled giggle. 'Control, assess, communicate, triage...'

The man on the floor shifted. His face was damp and the skin, a yellowish hue.

'I will move on. Is the victim walking? Well, it appears not.' Another snort. 'Is the victim breathing? Let's see.' The man's chin was grabbed roughly and held in a tense grip. 'I'm checking for signs of breathing.'

The man on the floor panted.

'No,' the figure said, releasing his face so it lolled to the side. 'Only minimal effort to breathe. I must act swiftly.'

'Why are you...?' The man's words were slurred.

But ignoring him, the figure was rummaging in a bag at the side of the room. 'For ease, I will not attempt any fancy, complicated heroics.' From the bag, a long cellophane package emerged. 'I'd judge you to be average weight for a man. Size four, I think.' The figure peeled back the clear wrapper. 'Try not to struggle. It'll be more comfortable that way.'

Hands were on the man's head. He thrashed helplessly from side to side. The figure, although slighter than him, pinned him down with a knee to the chest and began to insert the rubber laryngeal mask, pressing it hard against his clenched teeth. But still, he resisted. The nearest thing to hand was a heavy torch. This was smashed into his head.

He moaned but was finally motionless. His breathing was regular but due to tongue position, a gurgle sounded with each expiration.

'Airway must be secured.'

The rubber tube was forced roughly over his soft palate.

Perhaps half-realisation and half-reflex caused him to raise his arms. One last attempt to thwart his attacker. One last chance at life.

The figure smiled. 'And usually, I think we would attach the oxygen at this point, but in your case...'

The end of the tube was only one centimetre in diameter. Playfully, the kneeling figure blotted it, feeling the suction as the man desperately fought for breath. His nostrils desperately opened and closed but the attacker was quick to react, pinching a finger and thumb to stem this small opportunity at air. Finally, the end of the tube was pressed down hard. The man on the floor writhed for only a matter of seconds. In some ways, it was a disappointment that it didn't last longer.

The kneeling figure rocked back and sighed. 'Despite our best efforts, he didn't make it. Such a tragic loss to the world.'

D r Cathy Moreland smiled and tucked a strand of hair behind her ear. 'The faculty are pushing the boat out then.'

The woman standing next to her nodded. 'I hear it's their second year hosting it here. It used to be in a more central location apparently. I've no idea how they managed to book this on their budget.'

The woman, who must have been perhaps five years younger than Cathy and in her late twenties, put her leather overnight bag on the ground. 'I'm Martha Ross, by the way. Newbie at Auchterbridge. We're out in the sticks and I thought I'd better do something before I got called out to a nasty one. My worst nightmare. Not good with blood and gore, and the way people drive on those hairpin bends...'

Her voice was surprisingly low and emphatic. Cathy wondered if she had a stubborn streak. She reached out her hand. 'Cathy Moreland. Good to meet you. You're way up north then. Did you set off very early?'

Martha nodded. She was slightly taller than Cathy and slim in build but next to Cathy's fair complexion and grey serious eyes, she looked quite striking. Her skin was an olive tone and her hair, deep mahogany. 'Yes. When I got up this morning it was pitch-black outside. I wished I'd come the night before to save myself the ungodly start.'

'I'm only thirty minutes down the road so I had it easy. GP too,' Cathy added. 'I've been dreading this, to be honest, but I'm the same as you. I stopped at an RTA on the way home from work a few months ago and felt out of my depth. I thought it was time someone in our practice was pre-hospital trained. My senior partner wasn't for it so... Well, here I am.'

The two women stood with their backs to the great house. From their elevated position at the top of the steps, they looked out at the not unpleasing situation. The grounds of the hotel were quite extensive. Although mainly laid to lawn at the front, there was evidence of some clever planting, with several colourful shrubs and a line of tall beeches breaking up the otherwise flat landscape.

As she had turned onto the private road only five minutes before, Cathy had paused, her foot depressing the brake, awed by the beauty of the place. It was a typical Elizabethan manor house, simple and elegant in proportion with an agreeable symmetrical form. The two-story bay windows that repeated all along the grey stone, framed the square central columned entrance. The roof sloped to an open stone balustrade and above, six great chimneys stood shamelessly against an ominous sky.

As instructed by a wooden sign, Cathy had parked her car to the left of the hotel in a widened area of quarry dust clearly used for the purpose. She and her fellow course attendee had arrived at almost the same time. Approaching the building together, Cathy got a distinct impression that they were being watched. She looked up, following the line of wall that curved to the east of the building and was perhaps a later extension. In one of the first-floor windows, she saw a face, but before she could decide if it was a man or woman, it disappeared.

Now, at the top of the steps, Cathy sniffed the air appreciatively, as anyone fond of the countryside might, and thought that during any quiet time she had, she must come outside and explore.

It was a nice change from the routine of work. 'Off for a jolly,' James had teased when she had checked that he was still happy for her to attend. As senior partner at the practice, he had participated in his fair share of training events over the years and was clearly unwilling to upskill any further. 'I'm too old for that nonsense now,' he told her. 'You leave me to muddle through the daily grind with the locum. Come back full of enthusiasm and amusing anecdotes to brighten my week, Cathy. Then, when you have your certificate, if there is an emergency, I'll send you to deal with it.'

She hadn't replied but instead grinned and nodded. James's retirement had been mentioned in passing half a dozen times over the last few months. She knew he was becoming tired. The job took its toll on even the newest general practitioners, but James was now in his early sixties. Although he didn't often complain, he might easily have given up work a good five years ago. The practice had been subject to some troubles recently though, with the unexpected death of two team members. James had stayed on more for Cathy's sake than anything else. His retirement was something she dreaded. But they'd need to look for a new partner, that was without question. Stretched as they were though, even to obtain a good locum seemed a difficult task. Keeping on top of the day-to-day running of the place had taken priority rather than future-proofing for the inevitable.

'I wonder how many are coming. Do you know?' Her new companion asked.

Cathy sighed. 'It's a split-year apparently so there are only six participants.' She moved her bag to the other hand. 'My friend's one of the instructors. An A&E consultant. She's already in there setting up. Arrived last night for a meal with the other supervisors.'

The woman raised her eyebrows.

'Seemingly an ex-army helicopter medic, an advanced paramedic and her. We're being well looked after.'

'Three instructors for only six of us? It's a bit overkill, isn't it? I wonder who else is on the list of participants.'

Cathy shook her head. 'Not sure. We're starting in an hour so we'll find out soon enough. Shall we check in? I'm dying for a cup of tea before things kick off.'

Cathy turned and looked at the building behind them. The engraved sign was discreet but clear. Huntington Lodge Hotel. It was the sort of place that would be better suited to hosting weddings rather than an emergency life-support course. Cathy caught herself and inwardly cringed. She had only been seeing Chris for six months and things had moved far quicker than either of them had expected. Still, to be even half-thinking about wedding venues at such an early stage in her relationship with the surgical registrar was ridiculous.

The hotel was quiet and smelt faintly of furniture polish, which Cathy thought was a good sign. The carpeted hall was empty save one member of staff.

The receptionist smiled brightly. Her face was overly made-up and her hair was pulled back into a high ponytail. 'Dr Moreland, yes, we're expecting you. Welcome to Huntington Lodge. I hope it's not an issue, but you're sharing?'

Cathy had wondered at the faculty choosing such an exclusive venue, and this was the result. Still, she didn't mind sharing a room. She glanced up at the high ceiling and sweeping staircase to the right of the lobby. Through a doorway to the side, she saw the tartan thick-pile carpet continuing. No, she didn't mind sharing a room at all. She'd been nervous about attending in the first place and it might be fun to have a roommate to talk through the day's events.

'Who am I sharing with?' she asked the girl, whose name badge said she was called Andrea.

'We have you with another lady doctor. I hope that's all right? A Martha Ross. It's a lovely twin room on the first floor with views...'

Cathy turned to her new acquaintance and smiled. 'I'm not fussed if you're not. You don't snore, do you, Martha?'

The other woman didn't smile. 'I think it's a bit off. The faculty should have at least emailed to say. Surely that's just good manners.'

'I'm sure we could change...' Cathy began, looking awkwardly at the receptionist.

But Martha shook her head. 'No point in making a fuss, is there? It's done now.' She took the key card that Andrea had already laid on the desk and lifted her bag. 'Which way did you say?'

'Left and the stairs are just...'

Martha turned without waiting for her to finish. 'I'll see you up there,' she threw over her shoulder.

Cathy heard her footsteps as she crossed the next room and then began to mount the stairs. She shrugged apologetically.

'I can see if I can change things around,' the receptionist said. 'Usually, people don't mind. I know what she means. Someone should have said. Mr Faber will be about here somewhere though...'

Cathy smiled. 'I'm sure it'll be fine. Don't worry.' She glanced around the sunny lobby before following Martha upstairs. It was large and sparsely furnished. Although not currently lit, Cathy saw several low tables with lamps on them and she could imagine that come evening time, the place might look quite different. Thick brocade curtains of red and gold framed the windows which gave a panoramic view of the lawns and garden. In the centre of the hall stood a circular wooden table upon which a vase of white roses and purple thistles had been arranged. It was the kind of room that would welcome guests without being too ostentatious. Cathy was in no doubt that the effect had cost the owner a good deal of money to achieve.

The girl at reception smiled. 'I'll get someone to carry your bag, shall I?'

'No, not at all. Thank you.' She drew her mobile phone from her pocket. Chris had sent a message. It had pinged when she was driving and she hadn't had a chance to read it. Cathy smiled.

'No internet at the moment, I'm afraid,' the receptionist said. 'It can be a bit hit or miss here. Mr Faber was meant to phone the provider and speak with them.'

'I suppose none of us will need it if we're meant to be studying.'

The girl nodded. 'I meant to say, coffees and teas are set up in the Islay Suite. Straight through the double doors and on the right once you're settled.'

'Has anyone else arrived?'

'Oh, the couple are here. Two doctors, older than you. They stayed last night. Said it was a bit of a treat, taking an extra night here. Obviously, the three organisers are here also. They've been setting things up since yesterday evening.'

Cathy nodded. Her friend, Suzalinna had called the previous night telling her that it was a bit of a bore but that the place was 'nice enough'. Cathy wondered if she would see her before the course began.

The receptionist was still smiling expectantly at her.

'Are we the only people in the hotel?'

'Yes, that was the arrangement made by the medical director, I believe. You were to take the whole hotel with no other guests present. We're not busy at this time of year anyway so I don't think Mr Faber minded.'

'Still, it's a big place...'

'The scenario rooms, is that what you'd call them? They take up all of the business suite anyway so it would only be tourists using the bedrooms otherwise and as I say, it's quiet...'

'Mr Faber is the manager?'

'The manager and owner, yes. A lovely man to work for, although, I've only been here a relatively short time myself. I think he was keen to help when he heard that the hotel in the next town hosted these courses. Selfless, you'd call him. He can't do enough. Oh, I know it's probably good for business long-term, having you all stay. Some of the doctors might come back to the hotel again, and that sort of thing. But he has a particular interest in this anyway, what with his accident.' She leaned across the desk and dropped her voice. 'Lucky to still be with us. I think he sees this as his way of giving something back. Never stops telling us about how wonderful the paramedics were. Anyway,' she said, glancing over Cathy's shoulder, 'I'll let you get on.'

Not the most discreet, Cathy thought but a pleasant girl. She turned, suddenly feeling a draft behind her. In the doorway, stood a tall greying man in a dark suit. His face was pale and his lips, non-existent.

'Good morning,' he said. 'You must be Doctor...?'

'Moreland. Cathy.'

'Delighted. I'm Mr Faber.' He spoke with a slight inflexion and although he had a Scottish accent, she wondered if English was his first language. As he crossed the hall, he moved with a jarring gait. The receptionist had described him in positive terms only moments before but Cathy found herself slightly shocked by his appearance. For why, she could not say. 'I hope Andrea has taken good care of you? You are sharing with a Dr

9

Ross. I hope you'll have a relaxing but productive time with us. If there's anything we can do to assist you, just let us know.'

Cathy smiled. 'Thank you.' There was a pause. His sharp eyes seemed to dart over her as if in assessment. 'I'd better get myself sorted,' she said. 'Nice to meet you.'

'The pleasure is all mine.' He bowed.

Cathy lifted her bags. A hotel manager of the most hospitable character but for all that, she did not like him. Cathy knew that she was prone to feelings like these on meeting people. Sometimes the reaction later proved to be warranted but she had long since learned to be critical of such fancies.

By the time she found her room, through an anonymous but luxurious drawing-room and up not the central flight of stairs but a less flamboyant arrangement, Cathy was glad that she was sharing a room. The corridors on this side of the building were quite shadowy and the carpets a trifle more threadbare than in the lobby. She allowed herself to imagine returning to the room after dark and gave an involuntary shiver.

They had been assigned room thirteen. Although she had a key card, she tapped on the door.

Martha had already thrown her overnight bag onto one of the beds. She opened the door wide and gestured for Cathy to come in.

'Unlucky for some.' Cathy laughed, pointing to the number on the door. 'I've given myself the spooks already. We've only been here five minutes but I bet this place is really creepy when the lights go out.'

3

It was quarter to nine and determined to get her cup of tea, Cathy hadn't lingered in the room, only freshening up and making sure she had a notepad and pen. She couldn't understand Martha at all. When they had spoken outside, she had seemed so friendly, but in the room, she had scarcely said a word and when Cathy suggested they go downstairs together, the other woman had shaken her head.

'I'll not just yet, thanks.'

Cathy shrugged and left her to it. If she was sulking about sharing a room, she'd have to get over it. Cathy had been to several conferences in the past where the same had happened. She didn't particularly mind but then, people were funny, weren't they?

As she walked down the creaking staircase, her fingers glancing the polished metal banister, tracing its cold outline, she thought of her friend, Suzalinna, who must be impatient for the day to begin. Cathy wished she'd been sharing a room with her instead of Martha. What a giggle they would have had. She hoped that following the day's lectures, the two of them might get together for a catch-up away from the other course participants.

Suzalinna and Cathy had known one another for years. They had been in the same class at university and although a rather unlikely pairing, with Suzalinna infinitely less enduring and more impetuous by nature, the two women had bonded. Suzalinna had passed her assessments with ease, Cathy perhaps less so, but now, some fifteen years since their final year exams, they were still regularly in touch, both having decided to stay close to where they studied. Whereas Cathy had made a beeline for family medicine, Suzalinna had opted for the sharper end of things and had been promoted to a consultant position in their teaching hospital's accident and emergency department long before many of her peers had even thought about sitting the membership exams. Cathy felt fortunate indeed to have sustained the friendship despite her own issues, and even with Suzalinna's intolerance of anyone less ambitious than herself, she and her husband, Saj had been a great support to Cathy when she was diagnosed with bipolar disorder five years ago.

Cathy smiled, thinking of dear forbearing Saj, a pathology consultant himself. He would miss his wife no doubt, even for the couple of nights she was away. They had been blessed to find one another. Cathy thought of her partner, Chris, and wondered if, in as many years, they would still be as devoted, or even in touch. She certainly hoped so but then she had a habit of messing things up when it came to matters of the heart.

Crossing the lobby, she made for the door that the receptionist, Andrea, had indicated earlier. It was easy enough to find the Islay Suite as all the doors were clearly labelled. The business complex looked to have been an addition to the building perhaps recently as the paintwork was bright and the radiators, which elsewhere in the hotel looked like Victorian originals, were modern.

With her hand on the doorknob, Cathy suddenly felt nervous. Suzalinna had already warned her that it would be a long first day. They had mountains of theory to go through before moving on to the practical elements. Cathy knew by her friend's tone the previous evening that this would be as dull for the supervisors as the participants. 'But wait for the scenarios,' Suzalinna had teased. 'There are a few surprises.' She wouldn't be drawn though, despite Cathy's best efforts. 'I hope you're up to scratch, darling!' she had laughed. 'All will be revealed on the second day of the course.'

In the Islay Suite, an impersonal cavernous room with high ceilings and oddly modern office furnishings, Cathy found, not only tea- and coffee-making facilities, but two more course attendees. The man was sitting, swirling what must be the remainder of his cup of coffee. In his late fifties with flecks of grey peppering his dark head and a deeply-bronzed and handsome face, he looked up at her and frowned slightly.

Cathy almost missed the woman who was standing by the French windows. The dark green curtain shifted and she appeared from behind, a tall bony figure in a long skirt, with beautifully arranged grey hair and a pinched mouth.

'Finally,' the woman said, flicking the curtain behind her.

Slightly taken aback by this, Cathy crossed to meet her. 'I take it you're here for the Emergency Pre-hospital course too?'

The woman nodded and placed a cup she had been holding on the table. 'We were told to gather here at eight-thirty for a meet-and-greet, but no one showed. I might have had a walk around the grounds if I'd thought we'd be hanging around. Not a great start, is it? Not professional.'

Cathy smiled slightly. 'Probably hatching a plan for tomorrow. I hear the role-play practical element should be quite fun. My friend is one of the...'

The man cleared his throat and shifted in his seat. Cathy

turned. 'I'm sorry, I've not even said hello properly. I'm Cathy. Are you both GPs as well? My practice is thirty minutes down the road. I didn't catch your names.'

'We couldn't get a word in edgeways to give them,' he said.

Cathy had met men of his type before. Superiority and ill-temper often acted as only thinly veiled insecurity. She knew that she could talk too much when she was nervous and this place, along with the subject matter of the course, had already put her on edge. But she had no reason to feel any self-doubt and she would not allow his comment to change her sincerity. She turned back to the woman, choosing to ignore his remark, but saw to her surprise that he had flopped back in his chair and was smiling up at her.

'I'm Charles McKinley,' he said. 'This is my wife, Joan. We're GPs too, for our sins.'

'Ignore him being an insufferable old thing,' Joan said, now also looking more relaxed. 'He's a miserable so-and-so, aren't you, Charles? He didn't want to come on the course at all if truth be told. It was down to me and I'll never hear the end of it.'

Cathy raised her eyebrows.

'One last hurrah before retirement,' the woman went on. 'We're taking over the practice on Skeln. Have you heard of it?'

'The island? Isn't it off the west coast? Very remote. I heard they were looking for someone. It's been in all of the general practice journals.'

'Her childhood dream,' Charles said, rolling his eyes. 'And I couldn't bring myself to refuse.'

'We've been inner-city doctors for far too long,' Joan scolded. She smiled at Cathy. 'When I saw the post advertised, I couldn't get it out of my head. I told myself I was being silly, but it was on my mind all the time. So, I rang them up to ask a few questions, got chatting and thought...'

'She thought, why not?' her husband interrupted. 'And

dragged her poor exhausted husband along for the ride too. The health board jumped at the chance of two GPs for the price of one, of course. It'll be the greatest medical care the island has received in over fifty years.'

'I holidayed there as a girl,' Joan explained. 'Such memories. Oh, if you're after tea, it's the other flask. That one's coffee.'

Cathy had already found the cups and was helping herself. Tea from a flask always tasted rather plasticky but it would have to do. 'Do you want another?' she asked, but they shook their heads. 'Well, I'm guessing you'll be glad to have some emergency training before going there? It'll be a bit of a trek to get someone to hospital, I suppose?'

'Compulsory,' Charles said. 'They told us that at the interview. Not that it was an interview. More to check we weren't deranged, or potential murderers. We were the only candidates and they'd been looking for nearly six months.' He sighed. 'We'll get a nice enough house. The beach is two minutes away for the dogs. They've promised locum holiday cover...'

'It'll be fine,' his wife said, shaking her head.

He grimaced. 'The last time I had to deal with any of this emergency nonsense was when I was a house officer.'

'He's afraid of looking foolish,' Joan explained. 'But that's why we've come. We've lost touch and we've been spoilt in urban practice. Just think of the beauty of the island. I see isolation as a blessing. At least you won't be falling out with other members of staff. It'll only be us.' She turned to Cathy. 'When we're in the middle of nowhere with a three-hour ferry ride to the nearest main hospital, we don't want to be panicking over how to do CPR or put in a cannula, do we?'

Having squeezed the life out of the teabag in her small cup, Cathy came over once more. 'I suppose not. It sounds like a great adventure. This course is just what you need. My friend is one of the supervisors. She's in A&E, a consultant. I think it should be fun. We're all a bit rusty, that's why we're here. I was just saying to my roommate that I came across a car accident recently and felt quite useless. This course will help a good deal in dealing with tricky situations. A bit of a confidence boost. It's good to sharpen up our skills.'

The heavy door swung open and they all turned. A thin, pallid looking man came in. 'I'm in the right place? Emergency Pre-hospital...'

'Yes,' Charles said, getting up and dusting his trousers down. 'It's gone ten-to and God knows where the rest are.'

The man who had just come in, approached. He held a clipboard and fidgeted with the snap. Cathy looked down and saw the papers were the advanced life-support guidelines, heavily highlighted in places in luminous yellow marker.

'I'm Cathy,' she said. 'This is Charles and Joan. We're all GPs. We were just saying that we're out of practice with big emergencies.'

The man pushed his spectacles further up the bridge of his nose. He was tall, perhaps over six feet, but despite being probably in his mid-twenties, he still possessed the discomfort of a lanky adolescent, unsure of how to hold himself. 'Jamie,' he said, and Cathy smiled when inexplicably, his voice cracked, only emphasising her initial impression. 'I'm an advanced nurse practitioner in the borders,' he told her. 'Nice to meet you.'

Cathy nodded in what she hoped was a reassuring way. 'Martha should be down soon. We're sharing a room. Must be the faculty's way of saving money. She's in general practice too.'

As she said this, Martha walked in and there were the customary introductions.

'That leaves one more person,' Cathy said.

'They told me I'm sharing with someone but I don't know his name,' Jamie said.

The door swung open once more and they all turned.

'Oh, dear. Am I the last?'

His voice was deep and his tone, mocking. If Jamie was unsure of himself, this man was quite the opposite.

Cathy found herself considering his entrance for some time afterwards. Without question, at that moment, the atmosphere in the room changed.

Jamie, who had been standing beside her, fumbled and dropped his clipboard and Cathy was sure she heard a sharp intake of breath.

4

Angus McAlver's hand tightened on the metal rail as he braced himself. It came, as he knew it must, a low boom against the guttural drone of the engines and then the juddering impact. His legs stiffened and his abdomen tightened in an attempt to withstand the movement but it was too great and involuntarily, he lurched back, feeling the unyielding floor rise and then dip once more into the lowest point of the wave. He stepped forward, going now with the motion of the boat. Relax the knees. Silly to brace against it, far better to move as one.

The ferry that connected them to the mainland was the smaller one of two, only capable of transporting the handful of foot passengers that ever crossed and one car. Every other crossing was made by a larger vessel. It had been the larger one he had caught that morning at six, the first crossing of the day, and although that was one capable of carrying three vehicles, none boarded. Few needed transport on the island and it was better that way. The roads that had been tarmacked years ago were now crumbling, not because of heavy usage, but because of the sea. The sea did that to everything, it hung in the air, its salty breath clinging and eroding. Someone had mentioned complaining to the council about the potholes and the rusted road signs, but little came to the island in the way of outside help of that sort. It was left to the islanders to patch things up as best they could. As a rule, they managed.

Angus shifted his weight, feeling his feet damp. He stepped to the side and out of a puddle that had formed when the last wave landed. It would be a treacherous walk across the deck to disembark when they arrived. He'd seen a dodderer flailing and then losing her fight for stability a couple of years back. He had rushed over, helping the elderly woman up, parting her hair to see how nasty the laceration had been. Not bad, but scalps bled like pigs sometimes. He sat with her putting pressure on the wound until her son had arrived at the ferry terminal to collect her. Angus shook his head and smiled in recollection. So many encounters such as these had sustained him.

The ground heaved beneath him again and he pressed his hip to the rail. No, he'd have to take care when they landed. His legs, although he hated to admit it, weren't what they used to be and his balance was not as reliable.

Another wave reared up and the ferry's bow rose and fell. Few were making the trip with him save the crew and a couple of regulars. There never were many. Tourists occasionally came, but with Mull only an hour from the mainland, with attractive sandy white beaches, it was little wonder no one made the three-hour trek. He thought of the handful of passengers below. Out of the storm, but sometimes it was worse not seeing the sea in front of you. He would rarely go down there, even on a very bad crossing, especially on the way back. That was one thing he'd not deprive himself of. The first sighting. Still, even after nearly forty years on the island, he felt a thrill. It was like a storm surge, an almost physical pull. Perhaps he was becoming sentimental in his old age. That's what Mary would say. Now, neither of them liked to be away for long. The place was on your mind the whole time, calling you back.

He stared out at the vast expanse of water, so infinite it was almost impossible to believe that there was anything other than the sea. Looking down and seeing his knuckles pale against the stark white of the rail, he loosened his grip a little, although not fully trusting that the sea was done. He blinked as the spray rose again, smattering him and turned to look down the side of the boat. The paint all along had once been smart and clean. White on the deck and navy blue on the belly of the vessel with bold lettering showing her name: *Aurora*. Now, the paintwork was bubbled and warped. In places, telltale signs of reddish-brown shone through. It had borne the brunt of many a storm, that was fair to say. But then, much could be said for all of them. If you chose to live so remotely, it was to be expected.

Skywards, the clouds had darkened further. The rain started as a gentle spit, but within seconds it combined with the sea. He would be soaked through in minutes but it didn't matter. Despite the existence of a basic but covered lower deck, he wouldn't move. Instead, and in defiance, he turned to face the rain, enjoying its icy sting.

He was thankful Mary had told him to take his big coat. Although it was just past the best of summer, she knew the skies only too well and could predict from first rising, what the day might hold. Most of the inhabitants were like that, the ones who had been born there. They knew the tides and the weather. It came as naturally to them as breathing.

A smile twitched on his lips as he thought of Mary. Forty-eight years this September it would be. He'd promised her a treat, a trip to the mainland for a fancy meal but they both knew it wouldn't happen. Even a few hours away was painful. He knew she felt the same as him and it was a relief really. Had she not understood, it would have been all-consuming, the guilt of imprisoning her there. But it was the life they had chosen and neither regretted it. A lifelong service to the islanders and an eternity of memories etched deep in his mind that he would carry long past this existence he hoped. He pretended it had been a chore over the years, even to himself but now he had handed in his notice, it had changed. The bravado was tissue-thin. Mary knew, of course. He couldn't hide anything from her.

The salt of the sea stung at his cheeks and he pressed a hand to his face, the cold stubble of his chin a stark reminder that it had been nearly seven hours since he had seen his wife. Just a thirty-minute appointment on the mainland and it took most of the day. It had been a worry leaving her but she was quite capable and she knew her limits. Sometimes he thought she would have made the better doctor than he. She was far calmer in a crisis and probably more patient with the day-to-day things too. Having answered the phone and even driven with him to many emergencies on the island, he was in no doubt that she had more skill than many of the new medical students coming through these days. The last locum they had sent had been appalling. No idea about a thing.

He sighed. Every trip to the mainland had to be planned far in advance. It had been that way from the start. He'd been to his more needy 'customers' the previous evening to make sure they were aware that it would be a limited-service the following day. He wondered how Reenie was doing and hoped that Mary hadn't been called to redo her catheter. He'd pop in on the way past. She was in one of the fishermen's cottages just by the harbour anyway. Mary would know. She'd see the ferry coming in from the upstairs bedroom but she'd know why he was late.

'Only be another ten, Gus,' a man's voice called out. 'Been a rough one today though.'

He turned. The boat lad was grinning at him, his yellow oilskins were slick and shining, his cheeks raw. The sea crossing was as much a vocation for him as island medicine was for Angus.

'Aye, Malcolm. Not long now.' He nodded.

'They'll be missing you the day, no? Off for a jolly?'

'Something like that.'

Malcolm continued, his gait staggered and jaunty as a drunk despite his sobriety. Angus had known the family for near-on thirty years. Newcomers they still were but then that was how it was on the island. Unless you were born there, they saw you as an outsider. He was probably regarded as such despite being married to Mary, despite serving the community for forty years. He had delivered countless babies on the island and attended, in their final days, far more and yet they still thought he belonged on the mainland. If only they knew.

The sound of the engine had changed and when he looked down, the sea now occasionally showed a new colour. Inky black turned to navy and green. By the harbour on a fine day it could turn almost translucent azure, but not today. He peered out into the heavy, low-lying clouds. Not long now.

He felt it almost before he saw it.

His throat tightened painfully. An unpalatable lump. He forced himself to swallow.

The rain was now a steady downpour. It drummed on his head but he did nothing to shield himself from it. The engine roared in his ears and the smell of salt and diesel made him want to laugh aloud. They were slowing. The engine changed, a higher pitch now, almost a wail of protest. It would be a difficult dock.

And then, with his head still full of noise and his nostrils of brine, it came into view.

Skeln.

He was home.

5

B efore introductions could take place, Suzalinna came in, followed by the other supervisors. Cathy smiled at her friend who looked elegant as always but, Cathy thought, a little frazzled.

'Morning, everyone,' the man to Suzalinna's left said. 'I assume you've had a chance to get to know one another? There will be plenty of time throughout the morning. Sorry we're a bit late kicking off. I'm Kenneth Docherty. I've been given the task of coordinating the event today and tomorrow. Just a little bit of background so that you know about us. I'm a medic with the search and rescue team covering the north of Scotland. It's a job I love and I'm always keen to educate others. I've been the lead clinician on the training side of things for a couple of years now. These events are always good fun for the participants and hopefully trainers too.' He laughed at his joke, gesturing to his colleagues.

Cathy found herself smiling. He was a tall, muscular man and his face was florid. Cathy wondered if he drank. She was too far away to study his sclera. A tinge of yellow might confirm her suspicion.

'I'll warn you that we have a lot to cover,' he went on. 'I've had no complaints so far but we'll not be able to sugar-coat anything. You're here for a crash course in emergency care. This is not the place for the faint-hearted or the dreamers. You'll get out of it what you put in but we won't be held back by stragglers.' Cathy was slightly taken aback by this preliminary but the helicopter medic had clapped his large hands together and was beaming. 'Anyway, without further ado, let me introduce my aides. This is Dr Suzalinna Bhat, A&E consultant at Glainkirk General Hospital. This is your first year as supervisor, I believe, Suzalinna?'

Cathy caught her friend's eye and grinned. Suzalinna returned the look but the corners of her mouth did not lift. Cathy wondered what was going on. She returned her attention to the speaker who didn't wait for Suzalinna to answer his question but continued his introduction.

'Suzalinna is obviously well acquainted with hospital major incident management and team roles within a critical scenario. We're delighted to welcome her to the course. No doubt she will be an invaluable source of information to you. She's trained plenty of junior doctors and medical students in her time, haven't you, Dr Bhat? Let's hope this lot aren't too precious. It's a hectic couple of days, folks.'

Cathy glanced at her friend. Suzalinna's mouth strained into a smile.

But Kenneth wasn't waiting for comment and instead, turned and indicated the man to his left, who was balding and a good deal shorter. 'And this, ladies and gentlemen, is Duncan Hislop, a consultant paramedic and a very experienced member of the Association of Immediate Care. Duncan, this is your first course also, isn't it?'

'Delighted to be here.' He nodded. 'I think we've got a really interesting and fun couple of days lined up, folks.' His manner was confident and affable and Cathy felt that if she was in dire emergency, his face would be a welcome one.

'Will we make a start?' It was Suzalinna who spoke. Cathy smiled, knowing that she would be impatient to get things going. As Kenneth and Duncan stepped back, Cathy considered her friend. She certainly wasn't happy about something.

'We're through in the other room,' Suzalinna said, beginning to lead the way. 'I'm starting with a rundown on aims and providers, then we'll get into the scene approach and assessment.'

The course participants prepared to move rooms, collecting their notepads and other belongings. As she crossed to the door, Cathy noticed Martha's expression. The other woman had been standing just by the table and her face had a frozen look to it. Cathy paused in momentary surprise. Martha had surely been looking directly at the final course participant whose name they were still to learn. Cathy followed her gaze. The man, handsome with wide shoulders and a rebellious crop of dark blond hair, smiled broadly. She looked again at Martha who had now turned away. There had been a reaction, of that she was sure. Had it been Martha then, who had gasped when the newcomer had entered the room?

But determined to have a word with Suzalinna and realising she was short on time, Cathy didn't dwell on it. She had a feeling something more troublesome was stirring. She hoped that Suzalinna and Kenneth hadn't locked horns. Suzalinna didn't suffer fools gladly and if provoked, Cathy had seen her behave in quite a petulant manner. When she caught up with her friend, she touched her arm.

'What's wrong? I could tell a mile off you were in a huff.'

Suzalinna swept a loose curl of hair from her cheek. Her dark eyes displayed none of the wry humour that Cathy dearly loved about her friend and when she spoke, it was through gritted teeth. 'It's nice as pie in front of you lot, but those two were at each other's throats only five-bloody-minutes before we came in. It's been like this since we arrived. I swear to God if there was anyone I ever hated at first sight...'

'What, Duncan or what's-his-name, the helicopter medic?'

'Kenneth-thinks-he-knows-it-all-Docherty, yes. I'm sure he has one of those narcissistic personality disorders. I thought yesterday was going to be fun. A chance to set up and get to know the other instructors but after the meal we endured last night...' She looked over her shoulder and perhaps judging that she was within earshot, she shook her head. 'Look, it doesn't matter, Cath, I'll tell you later. We're in for a long bloody day of it. I can't see this going well, though. My advice is to keep your head down.'

Cathy was about to ask what she meant but Suzalinna looked behind her again. 'Later, okay? I'd better put my bloody supervisor hat on.' She smiled then at Cathy, a proper smile, one that lit up her pretty face and brought dimples to her cheeks. 'Later, we'll have a good gossip,' she whispered.

Cathy touched her wrist in shared understanding.

The neighbouring room was much like the Islay Suite but set out for the morning with a line of plastic chairs and a large screen at the front, showing the first slide of the lecture. Suzalinna walked to the front and arranged her notes while they settled themselves, each looking up at the screen.

'Whatever you do, DON'T PANIC!' On the slide, a cartoon doctor was doing just that. Cathy sat down and knew that within half an hour, she'd have a backache. The rest of the group took their seats also.

The man who had arrived last sat beside her and leaned across. 'Ryan,' he said. 'Ryan Oliver. We've not met.'

'Cathy,' she replied.

He pulled his chair closer to hers. 'Think it'll be an

interesting couple of days, don't you? Crash course in how to be a hero. Fun and games.'

Cathy nodded.

'You're a GP?' he asked.

'Yes.' She glanced to the front of the room and could see that Suzalinna was keen to begin.

'Me too,' the man continued, clearly missing the cue to be silent. 'What a laugh. Well, we're in the right place, aren't we?'

Cathy, now irritated by his lack of tact, looked at him; her brows raised.

He smiled disarmingly and raised his hands. 'Well, I mean if anything was to happen to one of us, if someone was to fall ill, or worse still...'

The light from the window highlighted his carved jawline and she saw by his eye a tiny involuntary tic. She watched transfixed as the muscle pulsed. For a moment, the room was completely silent as the rest of the group waited for the lecture to begin. Cathy looked away. Despite sitting by the heater, she felt suddenly cold.

6

By mid-morning, the group had listened to a good deal of the theory behind pre-hospital care and what might be expected of them in an emergency. They had heard about critical scene approach and assessment and had begun on the fundamentals of airway management too. The supervisors took it in turns to talk. Cathy was glad to see that Suzalinna's prediction of a fallout hadn't materialised and from across the room, she had only spotted one moment when Kenneth might have crossed the line, interrupting Duncan to explain a point. Still, no ill-feeling was apparent and the lectures continued, broken up by coffee breaks during which Mr Faber and Andrea from reception came in with flasks and biscuits.

'I'm exhausted already,' Cathy admitted to Jamie as Mr Faber passed carrying a plate of biscuits during one of the breaks.

'Come now,' the hotel owner laughed, overhearing. 'The day has only just begun. A chocolate biscuit will revive you. Perhaps the heating should be turned down. These rooms can get draughty so I had made sure...'

'Honestly, it's fine,' she reassured him. 'I'm quite comfortable.'

But as the lecture restarted, the room did indeed feel oppressive. Cathy shifted in her seat, trying to avoid the glare of the sunlight that streamed through the tall windows. In her peripheral vision, she saw zigzag lines and she knew that she was getting a migraine. When the talk on spinal injuries and immobilisation had finished, she got up.

'I won't be a minute,' she said and left the room.

Closing the door, she heard Kenneth suggest that they all take a break for a couple of minutes to get some fresh air.

It was a relief to be in the corridor where it was cooler. Cathy stood for a moment contemplating the line of doors to her right, each named after a Scottish Island it seemed. The door to the neighbouring suite where they had originally gathered had not been shut and she saw that already, the hotel staff had begun to arrange their lunch buffet.

Instead of heading straight upstairs to take a painkiller, she found herself walking in the opposite direction, curious to see where the corridor led. She passed the first room and paused outside the agreeably named Tiree Suite. The door was shut. Cathy wondered if all of these rooms might have a practical scenario set up within. She imagined the three instructors together the night before, devising problematic situations for them to deal with to test their capabilities at the end of the course. Had Kenneth annoyed Suzalinna even then? It didn't take much to irritate Suz, Cathy thought with a smile, recalling her friend's scornful description of one of her senior registrars only a matter of weeks ago.

'God knows where they get them from, darling,' she had said over a glass of wine. 'No confidence to make a decision and that's a dangerous way to be in an A&E department.'

A jagged line flashed in Cathy's peripheral vision again. She'd need to take a tablet soon or it'd turn into one hell of a headache. Before turning though, she read the subsequent room names. Two beautiful islands that she had herself visited as a child. Iona and Colonsay. The door to the Colonsay Suite was ajar. Feeling a little thrill of disobedience and knowing full well that she really shouldn't be snooping, she pushed it.

'Hello? Can I help?'

Cathy spun around, her heart thudding in her ears.

'Sorry,' she said, instinctively. 'No, I was just having a look. I didn't mean to...'

Andrea, the young receptionist, stood with a platter of sandwiches encased in cling film. Cathy was glad it was her and not one of the instructors. She grinned at Cathy. 'I thought you might have been lost,' Andrea said. 'The lobby's back that way. I've no idea who left the door open there. It's meant to be locked.' She shifted the plate of sandwiches from her shoulder, placing it on a dresser in the corridor. 'Gosh, I'd better get the keys. Mr Faber will be annoyed if he sees. I'm not doing my job properly today.'

'I thought these rooms were all taken by the course anyway?'

'Oh, they are, but we were specifically told that they were meant to remain locked. You know how it is, it's always the most junior team member who gets the blame and that'll be me. Not that he's like that, by the way,' Andrea added quickly. 'Best boss I've had but those were my instructions.'

Cathy nodded, not wanting to ask who had specified the instruction or why. Presumably, it was to do with the secrecy of their exam at the end of the two days. Suzalinna had mentioned the scenarios being a good test of their abilities so perhaps that was the reasoning.

'I was looking at the names,' Cathy said. 'I went to both Iona and Colonsay when I was younger.'

'A nice touch, isn't it? Better than calling it "room one" or "room two" and so on. I worked for one place in Oban where they used girl names. It was silly though. You'd be told to take something through to Sarah and at the start, you'd say, "who's Sarah?" It confused the guests too. Daft really. Other places do rivers and mountains but I think the islands are classy. A bit different. This is all new though,' Andrea said, indicating the corridor. 'Well, it's been done up recently.'

A dull ache had now started behind Cathy's right eye. She knew where the paracetamol was. She'd deliberately packed some in expectation of a headache. She smiled at Andrea. 'I won't tell anyone the door was open if you don't say you saw me looking.' Cathy laughed.

Andrea giggled. 'It's a deal.'

Leaving the receptionist to lock up, Cathy crossed the hall, her head now pounding with every step.

She fumbled with her room key but once inside she found the packet of tablets in her bag. She popped two pills from the foil packet. She'd need a glass of water. In the en suite bathroom, it seemed that Martha had already unpacked her things. Her toothbrush and paste were in the only glass that Cathy could see, so she rested them by the sink on a pink toiletry bag, also seemingly Martha's. Clumsily, Cathy reached across and in doing so, sent Martha's belongings clattering into the bath. She tutted and bent to retrieve the toiletry bag, her head thumping as she did so. Some of Martha's things had slipped out. Hastily, she collected them, her eyesight was distorted as the flashing zigzags crossed her whole visual field. The room seemed to darken.

'What are you doing with my things?'

She hadn't heard the door open. Still half-blind, she blinked away the jagged images. Martha was standing at the bathroom door, her arms folded across her chest.

'It tipped out, sorry,' Cathy explained. 'I needed a glass of water. I've got a migraine. Sorry,' She didn't know why she was apologising, but with her vision coming and going, saw Martha's brow was furrowed. 'I wasn't going through your things.' Cathy laughed, now annoyed by the absurdity of it, but still, Martha's mouth remained firm.

'You got your tablets? Just paracetamol, was it?' the other woman asked. 'You didn't need anything more?'

'Yes,' she answered, feeling quite sick. 'No, nothing more. I get migraines from time to time. I've not had one in a while. I had a feeling it was coming on all morning. The light shining in through the window... The chairs were uncomfortable too. I was...'

'The room downstairs was hot.'

'Yes. Yes, it was.'

Neither of them spoke.

'Well, I suppose we'd better be getting back...' Cathy began.

'I'll be down in a moment.'

Cathy left her there. As she went downstairs, she wondered what on earth was wrong with Martha. Anyone would think she had something to hide.

───────

The rest of the group seemed to have lost a little of their spark. When Cathy returned, they were just settling down once more but looked worn and bad-tempered.

Suzalinna looked across and she rubbed her head in explanation of her sudden absence. Her friend understood and came over. 'Are you going to last the morning?' Suzalinna asked. 'I did wonder when you disappeared.'

'I've taken paracetamol.'

'You should have brought sumatriptan. I might have something in the car. God knows why but I brought a bag of medication. I should bring it inside.'

'It'll be okay.'

'I've opened one of the windows and turned off the heating. Like a bloody oven in here. No wonder you've got a headache. The rest of them are wilting too.'

Cathy looked around at the other course participants as Martha came back in. Jamie was the only one still studying his notes. He had been sitting behind her. Throughout the morning, she had heard him sighing as he flicked the pages of his manual back and forth. They had been given handout booklets at the start. Cathy hadn't felt the need to write anything down. From her university days and having attended many courses in the past, she knew that she learned more easily by listening. Charles had been the only one to raise a question during the lectures, interrupting Kenneth mid-flow in what seemed a rather discourteous manner to clarify a point. Ryan, who seemed to have adopted her as a confidante, had nudged her leg with his own.

'Trouble,' he had mouthed and nodded across to Charles. 'He'd better not do that again. The boss man won't take kindly.'

'Anyway, this afternoon should be better,' Suzalinna said, cutting into her thoughts. 'We're doing practicals with you. Kenneth is doing airway management with half the group and I'm doing vascular access. I've got pig trotters for intraosseous infusions. Proper hands-on and get stuck in stuff. I even brought a few old chest drains, not that you'd be doing that outwith the hospital but I thought people might like to look. I think Duncan's doing basic CPR later on too. I told you it'd be rubbish going through all this but it has to be done. Tomorrow we do the scenarios. It'll be completely different then. The theory was always going to be a bit of a drag.'

Cathy smiled. 'Give me a clue about the scenarios.'

'You know I can't. Anyway, you don't need any help. You're going to pass no bother. We'll not ask you anything unless we've already taught you it today. Kenneth's room is a stroke of genius though, I must say.'

'Is it set up already?'

'Yes, so there'll be no sneaking and looking this evening.'

Cathy giggled. 'I almost got a look just now, but don't worry,' she reassured her friend. 'I didn't manage to see a thing. That receptionist girl, Andrea, ushered me away as soon as she saw me. Apparently, Mr Faber has made it quite clear we're not allowed down there. I suppose Kenneth must have spoken to him. All very strict and formal.'

'Right, everyone,' Kenneth said, moving forward and clapping his hands to gain their attention. 'Ready to get back to it?' There was a murmur of assent. 'Okay, I want you to imagine you find an unresponsive individual lying in the hotel lobby. Who would like to tell me the first thing you're going to do to help this person? How do you know if he is, or he's not, for resus?'

7

'I'm checking his airway,' Charles called out, scrabbling at the dummy's mouth and pretending to listen. His suit trousers had already creased but he had given up on trying to stay smart and, goaded by Kenneth who had told him to stop dithering, he had got on the floor, crouching on hands and knees.

'Well, go on then,' his wife said, kneeling beside him. 'Pretend we're on Skeln. You're meant to direct the rest of us too, remember? What do you want me, Jamie and Cathy to do?'

'Give me half a chance,' he hissed.

His face was crimson and Cathy wished she could step in and lead instead. She watched his desperate attempts to control himself. His hands fumbling and his breath urgent. She had felt that distress during her early medical school days. Back then, it was quite normal to be taught by humiliation on the wards of their teaching hospital. That was years ago but she remembered the pressure, fearing that a gap in her knowledge might be exposed. It never seemed to matter how much you studied, the consultant would always catch you out. Fortunately, Charles seemed to have settled though and was now going through the motions, albeit still not giving them tasks to do.

They had been separated into two groups for the last part of the afternoon. Following a rather miserable lunch, they had been guided through the practical stations, learning how to insert cannulas and chest drains with Suzalinna. Kenneth had explained how to manage an unstable neck and airway with a variety of different techniques, followed by Duncan, who had gone through how to lead a team through cardiopulmonary resuscitation.

Now, before dinner and running ahead of time, the supervisors had decided to give them a chance to practise a couple of emergency scenarios before tomorrow's main event. The Tiree Suite had been opened and the course participants were encouraged to take turns in assessing the scene. Many had been eager to gain the extra experience. Cathy wondered how easy some of them might find tomorrow's assessments. Already, Jamie had shown himself to be struggling. She had seen Suzalinna taking him to one side over lunch and talking him through one of the lectures from earlier in the day. In many ways, it was a relief when Kenneth didn't choose him to lead the first practice. Cathy felt sure that the young nurse practitioner would have frozen. When she had herself raised her hand earlier to offer, Kenneth had shaken his head.

Now, impatient with Charles's lack of leadership, Kenneth could not disguise his disgust any longer. 'You're the bloody leader, Charles!' He called out from the door where he stood observing them. 'I need to see you doing something useful. I hear you're headed to a remote island? I don't fancy any of the residents' chances if they collapse when you're on call. This is a critical incident, Charles. Give these people tasks to do unless you plan to do the whole resuscitation badly yourself.'

Charles looked up wildly.

'Your patient isn't breathing, Charles,' Kenneth mocked. 'You're the bloody doctor! You've been checking for signs of life for two minutes now. I think it's fair to say that he's unresponsive with no vital signs.'

Charles's face was beetroot red. He spoke through gritted teeth. 'Joan, you do the venous access.'

'I'll get the bag,' Cathy offered, stepping forward. 'I've dialled nine, nine, nine. Charles, can I attach chest leads for you?'

The elderly GP looked up at her.

Cathy felt a wave of stomach-turning empathy.

He smiled. 'Thanks, yes, Cathy. That's great.'

After that, they worked well and despite his faltering start, Cathy was impressed by Charles's knowledge and practical capabilities. Only Jamie seemed not to have a role in the team, but in his defence, Cathy thought afterwards, there were too many people in the small room and they were getting in each other's way. But if Jamie believed he had got away lightly, he was sadly mistaken. In his summing up, Kenneth was brutal.

'Room for improvement,' the instructor finally said, having decided that the mannequin had taken enough chest compressions. 'I'm sorry if I seem hard on you, Charles, but it wasn't a great start, was it?' He looked around the group. 'It wasn't only Charles I saw struggling. Please take note. We expect you to be of a far higher standard tomorrow for the scenarios. When it comes to the real thing, you can't be dilly-dallying around.' He turned to Jamie. 'Want to write that in your notepad?'

Cathy felt sick with revulsion. Why had Kenneth felt the need to single the nurse practitioner out in front of everyone?

Jamie looked defiantly back at his instructor. He was slightly taller than Kenneth and the older man seemed to be almost squaring up to him.

But Kenneth wasn't in the mood to be passive. 'Okay, Jamie, how about you show me how to insert a laryngeal mask.'

Jamie shifted uncomfortably.

Kenneth sighed with exasperation. He clapped his hands, making everyone flinch. 'Come on, guys. Wake up! This was taught to you only an hour ago. What's wrong with you?' He turned on Jamie again who had begun to pick up the wrong equipment and had a nasopharyngeal airway in his hand. 'Shit, you really haven't got a clue, have you? Hold on.' He left the room. They all stood dumbfounded until he returned with the other half of the group. 'Okay, it's a tight squeeze but I want you all in here.' They shuffled in, lining up along the wall like a group of badly behaved schoolchildren outside the headmaster's office. Suzalinna and Duncan stood in the doorway looking uncomfortable. 'Not good enough,' Kenneth began. Cathy was close enough to study his face and saw that her original impression had been correct. He had a slightly jaundiced look in his eyes. It was made all the more obvious by his contrasting purple face.

'I'm disappointed in every one of you if I'm really honest. We've given up a good deal of our time to teach you. Dr Bhat has lost two days of annual leave because of this. Duncan, well, to be fair, he was free anyway, weren't you, Dunc? But that's not the point. I've run these events for four years now and this is the first time I've seen such a pathetic standard.' He snatched the nasopharyngeal airway from Jamie. 'This is what?' he demanded.

Ryan snorted and answered correctly.

'Not everyone else seems to know, believe it or not. *Naso-*, meaning nose, Jamie,' Kenneth said cruelly. 'Look I'm sorry to single you out, but really?'

Jamie flushed, the florid pink spreading angrily from his neck upwards.

'Jamie, you've been taking notes all morning. I need to see the theory being applied now. Ryan, if you're so cocksure of yourself, show the rest of the group how to insert a nasopharyngeal and then laryngeal mask airway.'

Ryan collected the equipment and expertly demonstrated both procedures much to everyone's relief.

Kenneth nodded. 'Yes. In the real assessment tomorrow, I need you to call out the size of the airway first, but good.' He looked around the room. 'Listen, we're about to break for the day. We all need dinner and to wind down, but please promise me that you'll come back tomorrow with more enthusiasm. I'm breaking my bloody back trying to drill this stuff into you. The least I can expect is a bit in return.'

There was a murmur of agreement from the group.

'Fine. I don't like to end on a bad note. I'll hang around for the next half hour if anyone wants me to go over anything. We've given you a lot of information but none of it should be a surprise to you. It's not as if you're not medically qualified.' He turned to Duncan and Suzalinna. 'You two head on up and I'll see you after. Okay, everyone?'

Cathy was glad to be released for the day, and what an odd day it had been. As she joined Suzalinna in the corridor, Kenneth called over to Duncan. The other man was already leading the group out into the lobby.

'For God's sake, Dunc, be a sport and line up a whisky for me at the bar.'

Duncan turned and shook his head.

8

'Gus, dear? Is that you?'

It could only be him but she still sang out his name. After nearly forty-five years of marriage, it should have irked but it didn't.

'It's only me,' he answered, and having unzipped his dripping jacket, he hung it by the heater in the hall, touching this to see if it was on. It was, of course. She always made sure of things like that.

The house smelled of cooking. He inhaled the aroma like an asthmatic might their nebulised steroids. A homely smell. He wanted to fill his lungs with it. Something tomatoey, perhaps pasta, perhaps soup. She'd have kept herself busy that morning. Fielding his telephone calls first and if there hadn't been many, preparing a meal for his return.

Slowly, he moved through the house, unwinding the scarf from his neck. He paused by the hall mirror. His face was creased and solemn, his blue eyes tired. He forced his features into a smile but relaxed it almost immediately. You couldn't hide things from Mary, he'd learned that over the years.

The door to the living room was ajar allowing the cool grey

from the window to shine through, highlighting a line on the patterned runner. The floorboards creaked with every step. The whole house groaned and protested when there was a storm. It was as if it blamed its occupants for inflicting the elements upon it. Mary had often chuckled about it, speaking to the place and scolding it in the winter when many others might be fearful and jumpy. Up the road, in fact, one of the barns had lost its roof entirely the previous year.

But then, Mary had only known this. Her childhood home was now derelict on the west side of the island, the stone left to crumble now that the roof had fallen. The last time they had walked up there, more of the seaward side to the building had fallen. Tall feathery grasses and prickly gorse, honey fragranced and golden, had grown through. Mary had been quiet that afternoon. He knew it upset her to see. But the house, in truth, wasn't the vessel for her memories, it was Skeln itself. He had said as much to her when they had returned home. Holding her shoulders, he had turned her from him to look out at the coastline, the craggy shore with its pockets of silvery sand. 'It's still here. It's still all yours,' he had whispered into her hair.

Winters were harsh on Skeln and to an outsider, it was hard to see the beauty of the place. But people hunkered down and made the best of it. Gus still remembered the shock when he had first arrived as a newly qualified GP. A moment of madness, he had thought a dozen times of his decision to take on the practice there in such a cold and desolate spot. But he was a stubborn man, for good or for bad and he would stick it out. Before coming, he had already decided that to give it a real shot, he'd have to commit to five years. After that, he'd allow himself a pause, a chance to reassess. That moment had come and gone, of course. He met Mary. After that, there was no going back.

He pushed the living room door and smiled. She was seated in the high-backed armchair by the window that she always chose. The arms were threadbare but she had covered each with a rectangular patch of embroidered fabric. She was sewing now and looking up over her glasses, smiled. She pushed the material she was working on down into the side of the chair and turned. 'Well? That rain, Gus. I worried about the crossing.'

He went to her and bent, kissing the top of her head. Her hair had thinned over the years and was now grey as his own. It smelt of peaches and salt.

'You must be soaked through.' She looked up at him properly, squinting a little as she did so, her eyes were wrinkled and smiling.

'How's it been?' he asked.

She sighed. 'Well, poor Reenie didn't call so I assume things are fine. The Thompsons asked if you'd go over later though. I think one of the children was running a fever. He's in the middle of doing the sheep and you know how hopeless she is? I'd have said for them to bring the wee one down but she sounded hysterical.'

'I'll head out before surgery.' He dropped his scarf on the back of the chair and sat down heavily. 'Nice to be home.'

They sat in silence. The rain on the window came in bursts as the wind gusted around the building.

'Was it dreadful?'

The clock in the hallway sounded the quarter past.

'Not so bad.' He picked up the medical journal that sat by his chair. It still had the cellophane on it and must have arrived that morning.

'No other post today except that one,' she said, pointing.

He slid the brown envelope from under the journal and seeing the stamp, put it carefully down again. Not now. He'd look at it alone.

'I've made soup. Let me get a bowl before you do anything.'

She got up. It took her longer these days and she used the

42

chair for support to rise. When she was out of the room, he lifted the letter once more, knowing only too well what it meant. They had decided together six months ago. After his appointment today, it was now a necessity. He ran his finger under the flap. The brown paper tore in a jagged laceration. He scanned the message, his eyes darting to the salient words. 'Accepted the appointment,' 'start date confirmed,' 'Drs McKinley.'

He felt a draft from behind.

'I thought it was,' she said simply. 'When?'

'End of the month.'

She nodded. In her hand, she held a tray with a bowl. 'It's tomato and basil, Gus. I hope that's all right?'

He nodded. 'Perfect, Mary. It's perfect.'

After the turbulent day, the dinner that evening was rather dull. Cathy was glad to freshen up and change before going downstairs again, although the atmosphere in the room with Martha was still oddly strained. Thankfully though, her headache had subsided but she still felt oddly removed from proceedings. Perhaps it was the after-effects of the migraine itself or maybe she was just tired, but she found herself listening rather than taking part in the general conversation as everyone sat down at the dining table.

Suzalinna was positioned diagonally across from her which was a shame, Cathy thought, as they were still to have a proper catch-up. But they had known one another long enough to be sustained by a raised eyebrow and a smile of understanding from afar. Cathy could imagine only too well what her friend was thinking when she was seated between Kenneth and Duncan. Usually verbose and animated in her conversation, her friend was tearing a piece of bread and crumbling the remnants between her manicured fingers. She caught Suzalinna's eye and grinned.

'Not sure why we keep ending up next to one another.' Ryan

laughed, interrupting their private understanding. He nudged Cathy's elbow, making her jump and, unable to hide her surprise, she stared at him for a moment, uncomprehendingly.

'Oh, in the first lecture, you mean?' she asked.

On the other side of her, someone flicked a napkin. She glanced sideways and saw Jamie rolling his eyes. She wondered how amicable their room-share really was. Next to Jamie, sat Martha. She had apparently drawn the short straw along with Suzalinna and was by Kenneth who had already started on the wine it seemed. Opposite Jamie and Martha, were Charles and Joan. Cathy had already overheard the couple bickering in a good-humoured manner. She had wondered how Charles might feel after Kenneth's rudeness earlier, but perhaps Joan had told him to let it lie and to behave at least over dinner. Charles saw Cathy looking across and nodded. Behind him, Mr Faber reached forward and filled his water glass from a large jug. Both he and Andrea were waiting at the table. They delivered drinks to the group and took their orders with dexterous efficiency so that they were barely noticeable.

As Cathy watched the group, occasionally contributing to a line of conversation, she found her thoughts repeatedly returning to the afternoon's conclusion and Kenneth's wholly inappropriate behaviour particularly in dealing with Jamie, but also Charles. It had been so old-fashioned to shame someone like that. Teaching methods had moved on and there was just no need for it. Cathy wondered how Jamie would perform the following day with the added pressure of the assessment. But it became obvious that Kenneth had forgotten the fallout and was intent on enjoying a first-class meal and drinks, flanked by two charming women. He raised his glass, signalling for everyone else at the table to do so also.

'Everyone, everyone,' he said loudly. 'Just a quick toast to your good health after a long day.' His words should have been slurred given how much wine he had consumed. The fact that he spoke quite clearly supported her impression of him being a heavy drinker.

'I've been a helicopter medic now for near enough ten years. Ten glorious years,' he laughed.

Cathy felt that this was going to be a path of self-congratulatory monologue that Kenneth had trodden many times before. She looked at Suzalinna who was unable to meet her gaze. The corners of her friend's mouth were twitching and Cathy knew she was close to an explosive giggle.

But Kenneth was oblivious and he beamed around the table. 'Ten glorious years of what some might call heroics... I don't want to bore you with my vocation, but that is how I regard it. A vocation. A calling to save lives... Every one of us at this table has been called by some higher purpose...'

Duncan, who had thus far remained a jovial but rather conservatively obvious conversationalist, now cleared his throat. 'Thanks, Kenneth,' he said with surprising authority. He gave a half-bow to the other instructor as if acknowledging the presence of great authority and apologising for the intrusion into his anecdote. Cathy thought it was done very well. 'Let's all drink to that,' he said. 'And many thanks to you, Kenneth, for arranging the course so well. We can all see what an effort it's been. Now, who can explain to me why general practice seems to be so reluctant to have their nurse practitioners trained to the level of their doctors in pre-hospital emergencies?'

Jamie, who the question was obviously targeted at, smiled and moved his glasses up his thin nasal bridge. 'I had just been discussing exactly that with Martha here. It's an odd predicament and very backward thinking. I've been upskilled in every other area...'

The conversation continued. Kenneth looked for the first time that day, completely at a loss. Cathy wondered if he had ever been cut short with such skilful yet forceful civility. Now he had no one to regale with his tales of bravery because his two neighbours were involved in discussions on either side. He flushed and began eating again vigorously.

Suddenly Cathy heard Martha's voice. She appeared to be in a spirited discussion with Ryan. 'No, I can't say I agree. General practice recruitment is like a car crash in slow motion. But I can't see how making the entrance requirements any easier would do; nor do I see that opening up the floodgates from overseas would help. How many trainees from abroad do we have as it is? I'm not being bigoted, but we trained here. That makes all the difference. There are nuances in communication that an overseas trainee cannot begin to fathom. Cultural subtleties.'

'Do you intend to act as a trainer in the future?' Cathy asked. She would have dearly loved to herself, but given the instability of her practice and her own mental health recently, she had postponed the decision.

Martha turned. She had a quiet refined manner generally, but this was the second time that Cathy had seen her stubborn jawline. 'I think I'd make a good one,' she replied shortly. 'Why not?'

Cathy smiled. 'I wasn't being confrontational, I was curious. I'd love to one day myself, but I had heard that the applicants for registrar positions were declining.'

'General practice gets a bad rep,' Ryan said, languidly lifting his wine glass. 'Jack of all trades, master of none. That's what they say, isn't it? But when I see my contemporaries slaving on night shift still at our age, all for the sake of a bit of prestige...' He swirled the wine in his glass. 'Well, I think, crack on. Not for me. I could have been a surgeon. The GI consultant I worked for as an SHO asked if I'd consider swapping to a surgical rotation. I said no. I toyed with the idea of A&E.' He looked across the table. 'But I don't much care for all that virtue-signalling that seems to go along with it, or the work hard, play hard attitude.'

Suzalinna's eyes hardened.

'And anyway,' Ryan continued. 'I have a life outside bloody work. Being a doctor was never the vocation that it seems to be for others. I see no shame in that though. It pays the bills, as they say, and I'm an efficient clinician, even if I don't like any of my patients. No wonder half the profession seem to turn to bloody drink these days.'

Duncan frowned. He had already quietened one outspoken member of the group; was he going to step in again now?

'Seems to be everywhere,' Ryan continued. 'Damn alcoholics. I'm sick of seeing them in my room week after week begging for their diazepam or whatever else psychiatry recommend they try. Willpower,' he said, taking a slug of his wine. 'If I can drink and know when to stop, why can't they? If you say it's some genetic malformation just like they're suggesting about obesity, I'll laugh in your face. Excuses for laziness and lack of self-control. Nothing more disgusting than a sad old drunk.'

Fortunately, Joan stepped in at this point. The rest of the table seemed frozen in surprise at this sudden tirade. 'I think a good start makes all the difference,' she said warmly. 'If we encourage and nurture our medical students, they see the profession in a new light. It's a tough job and there are challenges along the way but I believe a strong mentor makes all the difference.' Joan smiled and patted her husband's knee.

'Oh, do you now?' Ryan challenged, leaning forward.

Cathy looked in puzzlement from Ryan to Joan. Ryan's remark had definitely been belligerent. And then she saw Charles, who had thus far failed to enter into the discussion. His face was flushed and his eyes were fixed and full of some unvoiced emotion. Cathy looked back once more at Ryan, who she had thought was grinning at Joan, but she was wrong. He was staring directly at Charles. Confused, Cathy tried to analyse what she had just seen. It had been only for a moment, before Charles had looked down, murmuring something to his wife. Cathy shifted in her seat. She was sure she had read in Ryan's eyes a mischievous devilment. But it was more than a teasing good humour she had witnessed. Instead, Cathy was sure she had seen amused contempt. In Charles's face though, something far more frightening had been present. When he had looked at Ryan it had been with unadulterated hate.

10

Cathy went up to bed earlier than she had intended. The alcohol on top of a stressful day had made her distinctly nauseous and she could only bring herself to eat a few mouthfuls of the impressive meal hosted by Mr Faber. After the odd exchange between Ryan and Charles, everyone had settled onto safer topics of conversation. Kenneth had a raucous laugh especially after a few drinks and despite Duncan's early snub, he found his way back to centre stage before long.

Martha, who had barely eaten a thing or touched her wine, was monosyllabic, as was Jamie. Cathy glanced across at them seeing that the conversation had petered out very quickly. Jamie looked like he'd rather be anywhere else and it came as little surprise when after dessert, he excused himself saying he needed to make a telephone call.

'Doubt he'll be back,' Ryan proclaimed loudly but no one answered.

Cathy thought that other than Ryan, they were all trying to avoid a scene. That's how it felt to her anyway. Having several big personalities in the group didn't help.

In the end, she stayed for coffee, more to keep Martha

company than anything else as the other woman seemed out on a limb. But when Kenneth announced that he was ordering after-dinner drinks and mentioned whisky, she decided to call it a night.

'I'll leave you to it,' Cathy said, smiling around the table. 'I had a migraine earlier and I'm done in.'

Ryan went to get up also. 'I'll walk you up to your room, will I?'

Cathy laughed at his blatant audacity. 'I'll be fine, thanks.'

Over the meal, she had mentioned Chris half a dozen times in an attempt to give Ryan a clear signal that she was in no way interested but he didn't seem to care. If everyone else wanted a peaceful evening, it seemed he certainly did not. But Cathy was too tired to play any games or to massage anyone's ego for the sake of it. She got up, turning her back on Ryan's pleas for her to stay longer.

At the door, Suzalinna caught up with her. 'Cathy, are you sure you're all right? You look a bit off-colour again. Is it the migraine back?'

Cathy smiled, suddenly feeling utterly exhausted and wanting only to be in her room with her head on a cool pillow. 'You know I can't do late nights,' she said. 'I won't be able to cope tomorrow unless I go up now. I've been feeling squeamish all evening.'

'Food was a bit rich, wasn't it? Listen, my bag's in one of the scenario rooms. I brought it in earlier from the car when we were doing the pig trotters. I had some out-of-date lidocaine for practising local anaesthetic administration. I should have buccastem if you want me to look?'

Cathy smiled. 'Honestly, I think if I get a good sleep, I'll be fine. Thanks though. Suz, don't let me ruin the evening. You stay and enjoy yourself. Swap seats and look after Martha.' Cathy nodded to the other woman who sat in silence with her arms folded while an eruption of raucous laugher came from the other end of the table. 'Look at her. She seems a bit lost. She doesn't seem to like me much but I feel a bit sorry for her.'

Suzalinna nodded. 'All right then. I hope you sleep well and we don't disturb you coming upstairs.'

Cathy left them to it. She didn't hear the rest of the group going to bed later that night. She didn't even wake to hear Martha coming into the room.

'Well, we'll start without them,' Suzalinna said irritably the following morning. 'I know it was a late night for some, but we did agree nine. There's a lot to get through today.'

It was ten past nine now and Suzalinna tapped her foot impatiently. 'No, that's it. The stragglers can make up a second group. Typically, it's just the girls who made it on time.'

'I apologise on behalf of Charles,' Joan said with a wry smile. 'He went out for a quick walk first thing to clear his head. He said he'd meet me in the lobby but he must have muddled up the times.'

'Kenneth and Duncan should be here though,' Suzalinna said, shaking her head. 'But anyway, we can't wait around forever. Martha, do you want to lead this one?'

Martha nodded. Her face was anxious but determined. Cathy had barely spoken with her that morning. Her roommate had showered first and gone downstairs; Cathy assumed, to allow her some privacy to do the same.

Suzalinna smiled now. 'Okay ladies, remember that this is a critical incident. You could have mass casualties. You know what to do in making your initial assessments. I'll be at the door ready to call out any additional information about your patients' conditions. This is only a practice run before your test this afternoon so there's no need to get too stressed. I don't expect you to be perfect and now is the time to make mistakes rather than later on today, or worse still, in a real emergency.'

'We've got this,' Cathy said, encouragingly, looking at Martha and Joan.

Suzalinna moved aside. For the first time, Cathy saw the name on the door. Skeln Suite.

'Oh!' Martha said, reading the sign at the same time.

Cathy turned to Joan. 'You're fated to do well in this one, Joan. Look, it's your island.'

'Oh, hang on a minute,' Suzalinna said and reached a hand round the door. She fiddled with the light switch. 'Funny,' she said and then smiled. 'No, that's fine. Perfect, in fact. Okay, everyone? In you go then.' She stepped back.

The room was in darkness. Martha, who was at the front, felt along the wall for the switch.

'Oh, I should have said,' Suzalinna's voice came from behind. She sounded indescribably smug. 'This is a road traffic accident and it has occurred at night. No lights. It's pitch-black.'

'Oh God!' Martha groaned. 'Why did I have to do the first one?'

'Please leave the blinds closed,' Suzalinna said, seeing Cathy move across the room to the window where a tiny chink of sun entered. 'The lights won't work either. We've removed the bulb. You might find torches if you're smart enough to feel around though.'

There was a chorus of complaints. 'Complete darkness though? Really?'

'Well, you didn't expect it to be a walk in the park, did you? Right, ladies,' Suzalinna said, ignoring the grumbles. 'Let's show the men how emergency management is done. I'm starting your timer now and I'll be watching what's going on from here. Just call out when you need info on your casualties.'

It was difficult to get their bearings with the door closed and to Cathy, the room seemed claustrophobic. By the thin strip of light from the window, she had already seen two casualties on the floor. Joan was walking hesitantly forward, clearly afraid of tripping.

'Stay there, Joan,' Cathy said. 'There's a casualty to your left. Martha, I think I saw the bag by the far wall. Do you want to look for a torch?'

Cathy had begun to feel her way about the room. She knocked her leg on something and found it was a defibrillator. Knowing that they would almost certainly need this, she shifted it to the centre of the room.

'Hang on, guys,' Martha called out in the darkness. 'Is the scene safe to approach first of all? I know she said it was an RTA but what if they've crashed into a power station or something? Wait until I get some light. For all we know this could be a trick to catch us out.'

Cathy paused, hearing Martha fumble at the far end of the room.

'Any luck?' she called. 'I think there are only two casualties. Joan's right next to one. The other was where you are, Martha, so watch how you step.'

'Here's the bag!' Martha said triumphantly. Cathy heard it being unzipped and then a flick as a torch was turned on.

'That's better. Oh, what a joke they were playing on us.' Martha laughed, swinging the beam of light around the room. Next to Joan, was one of the dummies that they had seen in the airway practical the previous day. It was lying face down. Martha swung the torch back and a second figure was illuminated. She chuckled. 'So that's why the rest of them are missing. Look! This is a big joke on us, ladies. See? It's one of them playing at being a causality.'

Cathy nodded. She had wondered if there was going to be a

surprise of this kind, given what Suzalinna had said the previous day about the scenarios being inventive. She had assumed that it must have been the lights being out, but maybe this was what it was about. 'Suzalinna?' she called out. 'Can we get information please on our casualties? We have two on the ground. We're assessing them now. Are either of them breathing?'

The door was opened slightly and Suzalinna poked her head in. From her voice, Cathy could tell she was smiling. 'Both currently not breathing, but when you open their airways fully, you'll find they have a resp rate of less than ten a minute. Right, you are safe to approach and assess fully. You're doing well. Carry on.' The door was shut once more and Suzalinna continued to observe through the window at the top.

Joan had dropped to her knees in preparation. 'That means they both need immediate life support, doesn't it? I'm doing head tilt and chin lift,' she said.

'Spine!' Cathy called out. 'That one was face down, Joan.'

'Bother. I got ahead of myself,' Joan said. 'That would have been a fail, wouldn't it?'

'Are you all right if I look at the other one?' Cathy asked her.

Joan nodded in the shadows. 'I'll holler if I need you for chest compressions.'

'Martha,' Cathy said. 'I'm coming over, can you shine the light this way? Thanks, that's it.'

They stood together by the figure on the floor. Martha moved the torchlight up and down the man.

'Oh hello,' Martha said, giggling. 'It's you, is it?'

In the patchy light, Cathy recognised Kenneth. A fine trick they had played pretending to be late for the course that morning and Suzalinna must have known all along.

Martha handed her the torch and squatted down.

'One of us had better shine this where it's needed for now. I'll check...' Martha began, but she stopped short. Cathy moved the torch so that it lit the man's face. 'But I don't understand,' Martha said, rocking back on her heels.

It looked as if someone had already begun a resuscitation attempt on Kenneth. Protruding from his mouth was a pale green laryngeal mask. 'It's probably been cut with just the tube left for him to hold between his teeth. Hang on in there, Kenneth, we'll have you feeling better in no time,' she laughed.

But Cathy, still holding the torch, felt a dreadful sense of unease. 'Martha, I don't like the look of...'

Martha was bending over him, pretending to listen for any attempted breaths. 'Oh, Suzalinna already said ten per minute.' She felt the man's neck but almost at once recoiled. 'What the...?'

Cathy began to take a step back.

'You all right over there?' Joan called out.

Neither of them answered. But coming to her senses, Cathy shouted. 'Suzalinna! Something's not right. Get in here now. We need proper lighting.' As she retreated, she knocked into Joan. Cathy continued to shine the torch on Kenneth's face.

Martha looked up, the shadows making her features distorted and strange. 'Oh God, Cathy, I think he's really dead.'

11

The door opened and a uniformed police officer came in followed by the divisional chief inspector. He had introduced himself to the group already before assessing the scene. They sat; pale-faced in the room that had been used the previous day for the lectures.

Cathy had only a sketchy recollection of the previous thirty minutes. Time and events seemed rather blurred. She pictured Suzalinna's face, determined and serious; her frantic attempts to revive Kenneth. Duncan had been in the room also although Cathy couldn't remember him arriving. His face had been almost grey and his hair unkempt. He shook his head. 'No use,' he had repeated again and again. As they stood in the semi-darkness watching in horror, Cathy thought that they all knew the situation was hopeless. Suzalinna hadn't been willing to stop. 'Come on,' she had panted, furiously trying to get any kind of cardiac output. 'Come on.'

In the end, Cathy had stepped forward and touched her friend's shoulder. 'Suz?'

The other woman flinched. 'Cathy, for God's sake get a line in him. Why are you all just standing there?'

Cathy's hand hadn't moved. 'Enough.'

She had never seen Suzalinna like it. Looking at her now, it was as if she took the burden of blame entirely on herself.

Chief Inspector Forbes stood before them and cleared his throat. 'Sorry to keep you waiting, ladies and gentlemen. As you can imagine, there are certain protocols in these sorts of situations. Clearly, we'll need to speak to you all individually to establish exactly what happened this morning. There's little doubt that Mr Docherty's death is suspicious.'

Joan, who sat at the far end of the room, began to cry.

'I hope you're not inferring that any one of us...' Charles began with an air of pomposity.

'Oh, shut up, Charles,' his wife said savagely. 'Just shut up! How can they know? How can any of us? He's just said he needs to talk to us.'

The uniformed officer cleared his throat. 'It's routine procedure, sir. Nothing more.'

Chief Inspector Forbes nodded. 'Indeed. Our medic is looking at things just now and then there will, I'm afraid, be a fair bit of waiting around while the scene is examined. Mr Faber?'

The hotel owner was hovering in the doorway. He had been surprisingly calm and it was he who had suggested the Islay Suite as a place to congregate while they waited for the police. 'Of course, we'll help in whatever way we can,' he said, bowing slightly. 'I can offer the guests refreshments while they wait? I will bring...'

'I'd like to go to my room,' Jamie said suddenly.

Everyone turned to look. He was the only one sitting alone. Even Duncan had positioned himself beside Cathy and Suzalinna.

'I'm afraid at the moment, we can't have people moving around the hotel,' the chief inspector said.

'I won't be. I'll be in my room.' The young man stared defiantly at the policeman, his eyes cold. 'That's unless I'm under some kind of house arrest? Obviously, if that was the case, I'd be as well going to the police station. If anything, I think I'd prefer it.'

'No one is under arrest. We're simply asking for a little co-operation while we get to the bottom of things.' The chief inspector smiled as if he'd dealt with many troublesome characters in the past and Jamie didn't concern him in the least.

'I can co-operate perfectly from my room,' Jamie retorted, refusing to back down. 'I'll lock the door, or you can do so from the outside for all I care.' He looked around the room at the rest of the course participants, his eyes finally falling on Martha.

The chief inspector turned to the uniformed police officer and said something quietly and then, facing the rest of the group, he spoke once more. 'I assume that the rest of you are content to wait here?'

There was a murmur of agreement.

'Excellent. Sir?' he said, addressing Jamie. 'My officer will see you to your room now.'

Jamie got up and stalked to the door without making eye contact with anyone. Mr Faber left also, ushering the pair upstairs. When they were gone, Ryan let out a guffaw. 'Thank Christ for that! Bloody nurses. Better off without him. What a drama.'

The rest of the group ignored this but Cathy saw that Martha's hand, clutching the chair arm, had gone completely white.

'I'll be back as fast as I can,' the chief inspector promised. 'Thank you for your patience.'

When the door closed, Charles was the first to speak. 'Well, come on, what the hell happened to him? I assume there's been some kind of accident.'

'How could it be accidental?' Duncan asked. It was the first time he had spoken since sitting down and his voice was odd. He cleared his throat a couple of times as if the words were uncomfortable.

'The alternative is ludicrous,' Charles said, his face growing red. 'Unless, of course, it was self-inflicted in some way? A prank gone wrong or one of these odd sexual practices...'

Joan looked skyward and let out a moan of exasperation through gritted teeth.

'I hardly think so, Charles,' Martha said. 'You didn't see the body. Where were all of you this morning, by the way? We were meant to meet at nine. Only the ladies turned up on time.'

Charles shrugged. 'Lost track of time. Went for a wander.'

Cathy studied him as he said this but he blinked and looked at the floor. It seemed quite clear to her that he was lying, but what might he have been doing that morning instead?

'I slept in,' Duncan admitted, rubbing his hand across his jaw. 'I feel awful now, of course. I doubt there was anything any of us could have done though.'

All eyes turned to Ryan who had yet to give a reason. Seeming to enjoy the attention, he grinned roguishly. 'Well, I had a later night than the rest of you, perhaps... must have slept in.'

'You were sharing with Jamie, weren't you?' Cathy asked.

He chuckled. 'Indeed, I was, Cathy. But sadly, if required, Jamie won't be able to offer an alibi for me, nor I for him.' And to her confused expression, he continued. 'I've no idea what Jamie was up to last night. When I made it back to the room, he wasn't there. Where could he have been? No doubt the police will want to know. I think the next day or so will be very interesting.'

12

'What did Ryan mean?' Cathy hissed after Duncan had announced he was going to get a coffee.

Suzalinna shrugged. 'I've no idea, but there's certainly no love lost between him and Jamie. It couldn't have been a worse room-pairing.'

Cathy was relieved to see her friend looking far more like herself. She had taken a cup of tea and had even managed the doughnut Mr Faber had personally brought to her. 'Something sweet for the shock,' he had said. 'I've seen enough medical dramas to know that at least.' He had observed them from the side of the room, smiling for a little while as she bit into it.

'The entire thing seems farcical,' Suzalinna said, the colour coming to her cheeks. 'What was Kenneth doing there in the room and how did he die? Was it an accident? Had someone tried to revive him but then panicked?'

'The thought crossed my mind too,' Cathy said. 'But why not raise the alarm? Certainly, if it was one of our group, they would have done. You drilled that into us for the entire day yesterday, after all. Call for help even before beginning resuscitation. It's not as if we're in the middle of nowhere. There was a phone at the end of the corridor and the hotel staff to alert.'

Suzalinna nodded. 'The only explanation is that someone bottled it. Kenneth's collapsed, they've tried to play hero, but failed to revive him and run. God knows why he was down in the scenario room though.'

'I wonder how long he lay there. Perhaps all night. I know you tried to help, but you felt him, Suz. The heating was on but he was clearly past it.'

Suzalinna grimaced. 'Horrible to think of him down there while we were tucked up, snoring. And then I sent you into that room in the dark...'

Cathy did not want to recall those appalling minutes. 'I'm guessing that like you, all the supervisors had bedrooms to themselves? If he'd been sharing with Duncan, at least he might have raised the alarm earlier when Kenneth didn't come to bed.'

Suzalinna nodded. 'Having a private room seemed like a perk, but perhaps it wasn't.'

'I wonder about family. Was he married; do you know? Had he mentioned anyone in conversation?'

'Divorced, I believe. No doubt the police will have his close contact information already from the hotel. That's one breaking-bad-news that I'm glad I don't have to do.'

Duncan was talking quietly to Charles at the other side of the room. Cathy watched with half-interest. 'He'd shown no sign of feeling unwell that day, had he?' she asked Suzalinna absently.

'Not that I remember. The police will rush a post-mortem through probably. It could well have been an MI given how much booze he was knocking back. But I still can't think why he'd have been down there. Do you think he had arranged to meet someone? Maybe he was fooling around with the scenario props for the morning in a drunken state.'

'I went to bed so early, I missed out on all the fun. Is that a possibility then?'

'There was a good deal of banter after dinner about the scenarios. I told Kenneth half a dozen times to stop talking about it. It looked horribly unprofessional, him gabbing off to the course participants about their test.'

'How was the rest of the evening? Were people getting along? I know you were concerned about Kenneth and Duncan. Didn't you say that they were bickering before the course began?'

'They were avoiding one another for most of the night so it wasn't that bad. There was a bit of a spat between Charles and Joan. You know how married couples can be? Everyone moved around after you left and Joan ended up sitting with Kenneth. Ryan went to sit in her empty seat. Charles looked pretty fed up with the arrangement. He was watching Joan like a hawk and I'm not a body language expert but he didn't seem too happy to have Ryan bending her ear. I get the impression they knew one another before coming here.'

'Oh? I thought that too. It was just a look after the meal.'

'Yes.'

'Who did you end up talking to yourself?'

Suzalinna rolled her eyes. 'Well, at the start I was between Kenneth and Duncan. You saw that. I ignored Kenneth and spoke mostly to Duncan. He's a nice guy. Sensible...'

'But easily riled by Kenneth?'

'We could all be accused of that, darling. I hate to speak ill, but he was an odious man.'

'I thought you were going to explode when he started on his speech about heroics over dinner.'

'Yes, well can you wonder why I ignored him after that nonsense? He was drunk and maudlin. Just enjoying the sound of his voice.'

'Duncan shut him up, though. I was quite impressed. Who did you speak to after I left?'

Suzalinna rolled her eyes. 'That Jamie is an uptight bore, isn't he? I chatted to him before the after-dinner drinks came. I dutifully listened to him telling me about his work and home life. Not once did he return the compliment though. Honestly, what a drag. He's got a chip on his shoulder about something anyway.'

'Maybe he was nervous,' Cathy said. She too became rather awkward in large gatherings and often felt pressure to say the right thing.

But Suzalinna shook her head. 'I caught him giving Ryan daggers when I was talking last night. He didn't seem shy and introverted then. Honestly, as soon as he realised that I wasn't going to give him any hints about the test, he lost interest in me and started trying to pump Kenneth. Odd, but not a single person here seems to have warmed to him, have they? And then, he refuses to sit with us even when the police ask him to do so.'

'Prejudice, do you think?'

'What, do you think we have collectively pulled rank as a group? We're all doctors and he's a nurse? I don't think so, Cath. He's just a frightful pain. Anyway, Duncan's not a doctor, he's a paramedic. We all like and respect him.'

'Jamie can't have been the only person you spoke with. Who did you sit with later?'

'Oh, I did as you said and spoke to Martha. She's all right as it goes but I didn't much warm to her either. In the end, I was glad to get away.'

'When did you all get to bed?'

'I'm not sure exactly. I left them to it and headed up. Must have been after midnight by the time I went up. Kenneth and Charles looked like they were in for the long haul. Martha had gone out for some fresh air but I did wonder if she'd simply made the excuse and headed up to bed.'

'I didn't hear her come in,' Cathy confessed. 'I was dead to the world.' Realising the misjudgement of her words she grimaced.

'Yes, it's going to be a bit like that though, Cath. We'll all be treading on eggshells. But someone here must know what happened to Kenneth.'

'A drinking game?'

'Oh, come on. Whoever was with him should have spoken by now. They can't have been so intoxicated to have forgotten that at the end of their lovely evening, they left a man dead on the floor.'

13

John nodded. 'Not much you can do, is there? I feel bad calling you out but I couldn't just leave her lying there. I feel awful now. Should have been up earlier but I was helping Lenny with the boat. God knows how long she lay for.'

Gus shook his head. 'It was probably very quick. She'd been failing for some time now. I'm glad she's at peace now. You should be too, John.'

The other man nodded and, wiping his forehead, turned away.

Gus removed the earpieces of his stethoscope and wound the piping over before placing it in his bag.

'I'll call Buchan's first thing. You know the score. They'll send someone across on the ferry.'

'Be lucky to make it over if the forecast's anything to go by. Sea pinars were enormous on the west this evening. When the waves get that big, we know we're in for a pummelling. We dragged most of the boats up as high as in winter. Haven't seen a summer one like it in years.'

Gus nodded. 'Are you happy to have her here tonight?'

'Of course. You're not taking her home to Mary now, are you?'

Gus chuckled. 'No. No, I'm not.'

He leaned forward and closed Reenie's eyelids, the tips of his fingers touching oily skin. 'There now.' The sheet was folded across her chest. He loosened it and lifted the edge. It rose like a sail and then settled across the dead woman's face. 'Never easy,' he said, standing up. 'But you did fine by her, John. You were an easy son and she had a good life here. The last few years were tricky. I'm sorry for that but at least she saw them out on the island. That's what she would have wanted more than anything. Not over on the mainland in some nursing home.'

John nodded. 'She was talking about him more and more this last week.'

Gus knew what he meant. 'It's often the way though.'

'Aye, right enough. As if she almost knew herself that it was coming. She'll be glad to be with him again. Took half of her with him when he went. She always said she didn't want to outlive him, you know that. Made him feel hellish guilty about it beforehand, do you remember?'

Gus smiled. 'It's the cruellest thing in the world, having to go on alone after so many years together.'

The younger man glanced across. 'I hear you're packing it in. I'm sorry.'

Gus didn't look at him. 'Aye,' he said, busying himself with his bag. 'Time to get a bit of peace myself.'

John nodded. 'Done your time, have you? That's about right. We've been grateful to you, you know? The whole family has, from Mum here to Sandra and the bairns. You've looked after every one of us at one time or another. Know who's replacing you yet?'

'A couple.'

'Two doctors? By God, Gus. That'll be a shock to the system. What'll the island think of that? Newly qualified then?'

'No. In a city practice beforehand apparently.'

'And you and Mary?'

'We're staying, of course.'

John raised his eyebrows.

'They'll take the place down by the surgery. It needs an overhaul but it's a bigger house and more convenient really.'

'Always funny when new folk arrive.'

'I hope they'll be welcomed.'

John smiled. 'Well, you know how things go. It'll take a while. They'll have to prove themselves to a few first before they're taken to properly. It was the same with you, no? They put you through the wringer, no doubt. Always that way with new folk.'

'I had it easy because of Mary.'

John nodded. 'True enough but they still made you work for their approval. It's always the same. Think they'll last then, the new pair?'

'I'm not sure. Perhaps. It'll come as a bit of a shock. Island life isn't straightforward and the medicine part of it is miles apart from what they'll be used to.'

'Thinking it's a romantic getaway probably?'

'They've been across once already to look and it didn't put them off. But they'll soon enough realise.'

Both men chuckled.

'Aye, and yet it does us, eh, Gus? It does us fine. And a nice enough place to live too.'

The elderly doctor nodded. 'A fine place to see out your days, there's no denying it.'

Collecting his things, Gus headed to the door. It was true what he had said. No better place to retire but if only it was that simple.

14

C hief Inspector Forbes looked hard at Cathy.

'Before I talk to the rest of them, I thought I'd hear your version of events. You have a bit of a reputation in these parts, I believe. When I saw your name on the list, I did a double take.'

Cathy blushed. It was true that she had had dealings with the police in the past. Non-accidental deaths in and around the town of Glainkirk had been surprisingly frequent and she had found herself caught up in their solution far more often than she might have liked. Still, she hadn't met Chief Inspector Forbes before and she certainly hadn't expected to be singled out. She cleared her throat. 'I'm afraid, in this case, I'm going to be of very little assistance,' she said.

The policeman nodded. 'We'll see. Can you tell me about the previous day? I imagine you've spoken to all of the people involved? No doubt, you have an idea of motives already.'

'Motives? Are we assuming that this was deliberate then? I had come to a couple of conclusions already but perhaps they're wrong.'

The chief inspector raised his eyebrows. His forehead was wide and intelligent.

'Well, my feeling is that one of them must know what happened. I think there was probably a bit of drunken carry-on last night. I'm afraid I headed up to bed early. I had a migraine on and off that day and I was exhausted. During dinner, a few too many drinks were consumed by the rest of the party...'

'As often happens at these kinds of events?'

'Exactly. People do tend to kick back and see it as a bit of a holiday. The instructors were socialising with the group and they were enjoying themselves just as much. I think there was a good bit of boozy nonsense.'

'Now, let me see. The instructors? Dr Bhat, Duncan Hislop and the deceased?'

'Yes. I'm close friends with Dr Bhat. We went to medical school together.'

'And no doubt you've discussed what happened?'

'Of course. Suzalinna feels awful for putting us into that room. We'd been waiting on the rest of the group to join us but they didn't turn up on time. We thought it was because of the late night before. Anyway, Suzalinna got impatient and said we should start before the rest of them arrived. It looked awful both Kenneth and Duncan being late too, but obviously, we now know why Kenneth wasn't there. But even when we went in and realised that there was a real body, we still assumed it was part of the scenario.'

'But Dr Bhat must surely have told you?'

'Oh, no, she was at the door. She was only there to shout out the condition of our accident victims and give us some guidance before the real test that afternoon. The rooms had been set up well in advance.'

The chief inspector rubbed his face as he thought. 'So, you

went along with the scenario, knowing that Dr Docherty was on the floor?'

Cathy knew it sounded odd. 'To be honest, it was dark and the torchlight was so ineffective, we didn't know it was him at first. When we saw though, we all laughed. It sounds awful saying it now, but we thought that the instructors had played a bit of a joke on us. They'd been teasing us about having a really exciting scenario planned for that day and we assumed this was what they'd meant.'

'When did you realise something was wrong?'

Cathy screwed up her nose. The memory was an unpleasant one. 'Joan was making a hash of resuscitating a dummy at the other side of the room but Martha had found the torches and I had found the defibrillator. I brought it to the middle of the room and went to Martha because she seemed to be having some problems assessing her patient.'

The chief inspector nodded. 'Go on.'

Cathy sighed. 'I'm not sure quite what happened. I shone the torch after Martha handed it to me and we saw he had the laryngeal mask in his mouth already. We couldn't understand it and then, Martha felt for a pulse. I think we both realised at the same time that it was wrong. I called out for Suzalinna to come in and ran to open the blinds myself. Once there was light in the room, it was clear that he was dead.'

'Dr Bhat...?'

'She tried to help. I think she felt it her duty to try, but we knew...'

'And now that you've had a chance to consider things, what do you think?'

'It's so hard to say, but from the conversations the previous evening and the banter going on, I can only assume that Kenneth had been drunkenly boasting about the scenario set up for the following day. I wonder if he was persuaded into giving one of the course participants an early look at the room that night. We were meant to be assessed in the afternoon and for some of us, the completion of the course was more important than for others. I feel awful even implying it, but what else can we think?'

He was going to speak, but catching himself, the chief inspector smiled. 'Please go on.'

'Well, there's not much more to say. I wonder if Kenneth collapsed, had an MI, perhaps.' To the chief inspector's raised eyebrows, she explained, 'Sorry, a myocardial infarction. Heart attack. I can't understand why the person with him didn't call for help though, but conceivably, they attempted his resuscitation alone. Failing to revive him and still possibly, heavily under the influence of alcohol themselves, they shut the door and returned to their bedroom.'

'Leaving the discovery of his body to the rest of you that morning?'

'I know it seems odd, but yes... that was what I thought.'

The chief inspector got up. They had been sitting at a small circular table in one of the free conference rooms. Mr Faber had graciously suggested its use, setting out chairs and a table accordingly. 'I don't like it,' he said, standing by the window. 'I'm surprised that you didn't see.'

Cathy couldn't understand. 'See what?' She dreaded what might come next. In her agitation, she continued to speak. 'The room was in darkness, of course. That was part of the scenario. That was the secret the instructors had been keeping all the previous day. They'd come up with this fun idea to make it more difficult for us to assess the casualties. They'd removed the light bulb and drawn the blinds. Suzalinna wouldn't allow us to open them. It was only after we realised something was wrong...'

'But you saw the body in full light after you realised? All of you are doctors.' He looked down at his notebook. 'You, Dr

Suzalinna Bhat, Dr Martha Ross and Dr Joan McKinley. Four doctors.'

Cathy swallowed. The room seemed still but for the thud of her heart. 'I assume you mean his eyes? His face?'

The chief inspector didn't speak.

'He had been drinking. If you're referring to the blood vessels...?'

'Our police medic called them petechiae. He spotted them as soon as he looked at the dead man.'

'To be fair, I'm not experienced in these things. I think he had a long-standing alcohol problem. Before that night, I'd noticed he had spider telangiectasis on his arms and neck also. He was mildly jaundiced too. It might easily have been that.'

'Or it might have been...'

The room was silent. Cathy swallowed.

'Asphyxia?' Her voice wavered. The suggestion was quite appalling.

The chief inspector didn't answer but sat down once more. 'Anyway, there's no point in jumping to conclusions yet.' His voice was overly jovial. 'The post-mortem will reveal the cause of death soon enough. But supposing things had been as you suggest. Is there anyone in the group who might have panicked and left him, having already tried but failed to help?'

Cathy shook her head but she had already considered the one candidate who seemed more desperate to pass than the rest, who had also reacted unusually, not wanting to sit with the others. It didn't seem fair to pick Jamie out but it did all lead to him.

The chief inspector seemed to realise her difficulty. 'I can see that it's an unfair question,' he smiled, 'but you mentioned the course being important to several individuals? Some more so than others?'

Cathy nodded. 'I don't suppose it's any kind of a secret that

Charles and Joan need to get the certificate so they can take up a partnership position. Jamie did seem keen to pass, but I think it was more for his satisfaction than anything other than that. Martha and I had no urgency to be here, and as for Ryan, I have no idea what he wanted from the two days. Over the meal last night, he made it quite clear that he found the whole thing a bore.'

The chief inspector leaned back and sighed. 'Perhaps, given time, someone will come forward of their own accord with information. I can see it will be a difficult investigation. You are all intelligent and, if I may say so, guarded individuals.'

'If I can help at all, I will. I don't mean to be evasive...'

'No, of course. Perhaps I will ask for your help though. I could do with a translator of sorts.'

Cathy raised her eyebrows.

'The medical jargon. Perhaps you'll put the others at their ease also.'

She nodded. 'Only too happy. I hope it will be cleared up quickly.'

'Clearly, if there has been an accident and this individual failed to raise the alarm, questions will need to be answered... Still, one would think it preferable to an intrusive police investigation. After all, people want to get home, no doubt. I can hardly allow anyone to do so yet, with a potential non-accidental death on our hands. For the time being anyway, everyone will have to stay at Huntington Lodge Hotel.'

15

'No. I'm not sorry he's dead. There, I've said it.'

Cathy shifted in her seat. The chief inspector had asked her to stay and she sat as unobtrusively as possible at the side of the room. Duncan shot her a look as he was led in by the uniformed officer. Gone was the affable good humour that she had seen the previous night. Now, he looked like a frightened man and in Cathy's experience, when afraid, people often lashed out.

'Dr Moreland is staying at my request,' the chief inspector had explained at the start. 'That's if you have no objection?'

'I have no objection,' he said. 'Why would I? None at all. Nothing I have to say is confidential or groundbreaking.' He looked at Cathy. 'You saw even in the twenty-four hours that you knew him that he was a difficult man.' Cathy didn't comment and Duncan continued, turning then to the chief inspector. 'The way he spoke to the course participants was a disgrace. That kind of teaching went out with the ark.'

Chief Inspector Forbes cleared his throat.

'Teaching by humiliation,' Duncan explained. 'He was pretty much the same in dealing with the other instructors too. You're friendly with Dr Bhat, aren't you?' he asked, suddenly turning to Cathy. His eyes were bloodshot and his face, pale.

She nodded. 'Yes. We've known one another since medical school.'

'I suppose she's told you what Kenneth said to her the night before the course?'

Cathy shook her head. 'I don't think I...'

Duncan shook his head. 'There's more than just myself who will be glad to see the back of him.'

'I have to say, I'm surprised...' the chief inspector began.

'Oh, highly improper to voice it, but you did ask.'

'Your honesty is quite refreshing. I hope the rest are as candid as you. Can you tell me about the meal yesterday evening? I hear that there was a good deal of joking around, shall we say, about the scenario rooms? These were where you planned to assess the course participants the next day, is that right?'

'We did the theory and some of the practical stuff on day one. Day two was for ironing out scenarios before the participants were tested in the afternoon. I had come up with half a dozen suggestions for the rooms. I'd been emailing Kenneth about it long before the course. I heard about a set-up down south where they'd managed an outside accident scene. They had the casualties trapped in a car and the course participants went through the assessment dealing with the safe extrication of them. I thought it would be an excellent test. Something a bit different.'

'This was your first course as an instructor?'

'Yes. I'd been warned about Kenneth though.' He rolled his eyes. 'In medical circles, word gets around. He was well known to be a pig-headed so-and-so. He replied to the first email I sent in a friendly enough way, but it was clear he was the lead instructor and he would have the final say. I thought it would be fun to shake things up a bit and try the outside accident, but he wasn't for it. Said he'd had another idea that would test the candidates far better.'

'So, the darkened room was Kenneth's idea?'

Duncan nodded. 'Proud as punch he was and it was a good idea really. I just didn't like the way he had belittled me and Dr Bhat.'

'He was a helicopter medic, I believe? Used to dealing with the sharper end of things?'

'I'm not denying that he was a highly skilled man. He had dozens of heroic tales to tell after a few drinks. Ludicrous really in our company.'

The chief inspector didn't speak but raised his expressive eyebrows once more.

'Oh, I just mean, why boast when we did the same bloody thing? Dr Bhat runs the local A&E department, for God's sake. I'm a consultant paramedic. I know I don't have a medical degree but I've studied far more years than most of the doctors here have done. I don't go around bragging about all the folk I've saved though. Ridiculous really.'

'Back to that evening.'

Duncan grimaced. 'It had been a trying day. Mostly due to Kenneth's way of dealing with things. A few people drank too much with the meal, none more so than Kenneth himself.'

'And you? Were you drinking that night?'

'No. It was a work event. It would have been totally inappropriate.'

'Go on.'

Duncan sighed. 'If you're wanting to know what happened to Kenneth after the meal, you're asking the wrong man. Admittedly, I did stay up later than some. In a way, it was to keep an eye on things. I didn't like Kenneth's attitude and I liked it even less when he was intoxicated. He was behaving quite unprofessionally and as a new lead instructor I saw it as my duty, I suppose, to keep an eye on things. If Kenneth couldn't look after his trainees, I felt I should. Besides anything else, we all had to be up in the morning. As it got later, I decided to give it up. I didn't fancy teaching and assessing the next day with no sleep at all.'

'Or a raging hangover,' the chief inspector said, but his gentle attempt at humour fell flat.

Duncan frowned and folded his arms across his chest. 'Hardly. As I said, I wasn't drinking.'

The police detective nodded. 'Of course. And what time did you go to bed?'

'At a guess, it must have been a little after half eleven, although I can't be sure.'

'And that left who still up?'

'When I went up to the room, Kenneth had ordered another whisky for himself, Charles and Ryan. Martha was in the lobby when I passed. I asked her if she was all right. I'd thought she had gone up ages before.'

Cathy, who had been studying her hands, looked up.

'Oh?' the chief inspector asked, also interested.

'Funny, now I think about it,' Duncan said. 'She did look a little odd. I can't explain really. I suppose I was wanting to get up to bed and I only passed her. She didn't say much. Just that she was getting a breath of fresh air. As I say, I thought she'd gone to bed long before.'

'She was alone in the lobby?'

'That's right.'

Cathy wondered if the chief inspector was questioning the same as she. The corridor that led to the scenario rooms was directly off the lobby. But what had Martha been doing if she was there? Surely, she hadn't needed to cheat and get a look ahead of their assessments. Cathy had practised intubation skills alongside Martha that previous day and the other woman was quite competent.

She coughed. 'I assume Joan had gone up already, Duncan?'

He turned to her. 'Not long after you left, Cathy. I don't blame you, by the way. You were stuck next to that Jamie fellow for half the night and he looked hard work. It was a difficult group to manage on the whole. Different personalities, I suppose.'

Cathy smiled slightly. 'And Jamie?'

'Oh, he went up around the same time as Joan, I think. Said he wanted to look over some of his notes before turning in. He took it all very seriously. I admired his dedication but I did see that he was a little out of his depth. It was almost as if he wanted to keep himself a bit distant from everyone. Perhaps he's simply a shy, private sort of man.'

Cathy remembered what Ryan had said earlier about Jamie not being in the room even when he returned late. What had the nurse practitioner been doing and where had he been?

'And when you went up, Kenneth was...' began the chief inspector.

'Kenneth was very much alive,' Duncan concluded. 'Alive and kicking. When I went to bed, he was off on one of his bloody anecdotes. Christ knows why Charles and Ryan were listening to it. All we heard about was his bravery. Ironic really.'

'Oh?' the chief inspector asked.

'From what he said, he could have died a hundred times over in the line of duty. Hanging out the side of a helicopter, lifting folk from mountains or the sea. Told us about all his near-misses. Funny to think of him, no better than a common alcoholic, ending his days drunk on a grubby hotel floor.'

As Duncan got up to leave Cathy wondered why he hadn't mentioned shutting Kenneth down at the dinner table earlier in the evening. Kenneth had been about to make a great speech but Duncan had been the one to stop it. He had been quite impressively forceful too. If he was to be believed, later on that night, Duncan had given up any attempts to quieten the other instructor and gone to bed, leaving Kenneth to his gallant tales and his whisky. Cathy wondered if he had done this deliberately, hoping that Kenneth might hang himself, so to speak. Everyone at the table the previous night must surely have known that Kenneth had an alcohol problem, after all. Had Duncan hoped he might drink himself into a stupor? Had he planned to take on the role of lead instructor himself in the morning while Kenneth lay disgraced and incapacitated in his room?

Whatever the case, Cathy didn't like what Duncan had said, but more than that, she hadn't liked his manner. Something had changed. Glancing at the chief inspector who showed Duncan to the door, she could tell he felt much the same.

16

'So, Dr Moreland, what do you say to that?'

Cathy looked unhappily at the chief inspector. 'I'm as shocked as you. He's so full of anger. I knew that he and Kenneth had locked horns, but the way he spoke about him just now was...'

'Yes. I wonder what the rest of them thought of the dead man. It sounds like he ruffled a few feathers. What did he mean about your friend, Dr Bhat, by the way? He suggested that Dr Docherty had insulted or antagonised her the night before the course began. Any idea what that was all about?'

'I couldn't say. She never mentioned it. She's spoken to me about Kenneth and Duncan's dislike for one another and the awkwardness of the whole set-up, but she never said anything in particular about herself. I must say, Suzalinna's pretty thick-skinned if Kenneth had been troublesome though. Whereas Duncan seems not to be the type to be rattled by criticism, she would only stand taller and fight her corner. She's good at her job and she knows it. She's not easily upset.' Even as she said the words, Cathy recalled her friend's attitude when she walked in with Kenneth and Duncan on the first day. She had indeed been bothered and she, Cathy had essentially just lied to the chief inspector. She swallowed and looked at her hands.

'I see. And if we still go on your supposition that this was a failed resuscitation...'

'Well,' she hurriedly continued. 'Here's what might have happened: as we just saw, Duncan could well be the one to lose the most if he didn't cope under pressure. He's an instructor, after all, a consultant paramedic. If he tried to help a collapsed Kenneth and messed the thing up, and on top of that he ran off, it would look awful. He admits that he was one of the last men standing that night. Perhaps Ryan and Charles can corroborate what he says about going to bed earlier than them, but even that doesn't count for much. He was alone in his room, as were all the instructors. Who's to say, that instead of going to bed, he went down again to speak with Kenneth later on?'

The chief inspector nodded. 'Tricky, I agree. It sounds like people may have gone up to bed, but not stayed there. I was interested in what he said about Dr Ross in the lobby...'

'We're sharing a room so I feel I ought to be more help with this, but I honestly can't say I heard Martha come in. I don't know what was wrong with me that night. The hotel was far too hot and I ended up with a bad migraine in the morning.'

The chief inspector nodded for her to continue.

'Well, I took a couple of paracetamol and, not wanting to miss anything, went back downstairs for the rest of the lectures. I felt a bit washed out all afternoon but by evening I was all right and joined everyone for the meal. It was only during the starter that I began to flag again. I knew I couldn't stay up late but the headache put an end to even waiting for coffee. I must have gone up at ten thirty. I was out like a light by eleven. I missed Martha coming into the room completely.'

'What is Dr Ross like? I assume you've become acquainted

having shared a room? How did she get on with the dead man? You probably know her better than most.'

Cathy shrugged. 'You say that, but I'd have to disagree. I don't think she was particularly happy to find out we were sharing. When I met her, I thought we'd get on, but she went a bit cold and I've barely said more than a few words to her in the room. There was a bit of awkwardness getting changed for dinner and sharing a bathroom. I went to Suzalinna's room for a pre-dinner chat just to get out of her way really.'

'So, you've no idea what she might have seen to make her behave oddly that night? No idea why she might have still been downstairs when everyone thought she had gone up to bed?'

'Honestly, I couldn't tell you.' Cathy shook her head and looked apologetically at the chief inspector.

'Perhaps we should find out. Are you still comfortable sitting in?'

Cathy nodded. 'Of course. But I doubt she'll allow it. I get the impression that Martha likes to keep her cards close to her chest. If you ask, she'll say no.'

Martha glared when the question was posed. 'Why on earth?'

'Dr Moreland has been of great assistance to the police in the past. I'm grateful for her advice on the medical side of things here. If you'd rather she stepped outside...'

'I would.' She looked at Cathy and forced a smile. 'No offence meant, but I can't imagine why you would be of particular assistance to the police in interpreting what I have to say. I'm happy to use non-medical lingo if that's what you're afraid of, chief inspector.' This she said with a little bark of a laugh.

Cathy got up. 'Not a problem.' As she pulled the door closed, she exchanged a look with the chief inspector to say 'told you so.'

Now in the lobby, Cathy wondered what she should do. Hanging around outside the interview room seemed a little too much like she was attempting to eavesdrop. She'd probably be expected to return to the other room with the rest of the course participants. She looked at the clock on the wall. It was almost one. The morning seemed to have passed so quickly. No one would mind if she returned to her bedroom briefly to freshen up. The one thing she wanted above all else was to splash cold water on her face.

She passed quickly through the lobby. It was hard not to be drawn into looking down the corridor that led to the scenario rooms. A group of suited men were standing at the door to the room where Kenneth had been found. Presumably, they'd moved the body by now and were examining the corridor and room he had been found in. She paused, wondering what the post-mortem might show. If the chief inspector was right and her theory of a failed resuscitation was incorrect, the only alternative was murder. She shuddered. *Please don't let it be so.* If only one of the course participants would own up to having made a mistake. A moment of drunken poor judgement. If they did so, this whole thing would be concluded. But she wasn't a fool. If they hadn't spoken by now, it would be highly unlikely that anyone would confess now.

She turned as one of the suited men began to walk towards her. She'd nip upstairs for just a moment. But she was startled. Mr Faber stood in front of her.

'Dr Moreland,' he smiled, 'not running away, I hope? And I'd so wanted a little word.'

17

It only took her a second to recover. 'Mr Faber,' she smiled. 'You made me jump.'

He nodded and beamed disarmingly. 'I'm all apologies. We are a little shaken by things today, I feel.'

'Oh yes. I'm afraid it will make things rather awkward for the hotel.'

He waved a hand, dismissing the comment. 'We will try to co-operate with the police as best we can. Accommodating and ensuring our remaining guests are as comfortable as possible is a priority still.'

'Right.' Cathy didn't like the 'remaining guests' comment but he hadn't meant anything by it. 'I was just going up to my room to freshen up. But as you're here, I had wondered...'

'Yes? Anything I can do for you, doctor.'

She wasn't planning to ask him anything, but he had been there last night, along with the rest of them. Could Mr Faber have seen anything of importance?

'It's nothing really,' she said. 'I did just wonder about last night though. I realise that we were keeping the hotel staff up quite late with our meal and after-dinner drinks...'

'You're asking if I know what happened to the poor man?'

'I suppose so. I realise the chief inspector has probably already been through it with you. I just thought that if one of the staff had seen something...'

He nodded. 'I think we all want to find out what happened as much as each other. You're quite correct. I have spoken to the chief inspector already. I'm happy to tell you what I told him. I was attending to the evening, myself, as you know. When we have a small but important group, I like to host rather than leave it to the more junior members of staff.'

Cathy nodded. 'You were very attentive over the meal. I wondered if afterwards...?'

Mr Faber flashed his white teeth and nodded. 'Yes, yes. Quite right. I don't often feel the need to stay up for drinks. Andrea was quite in control of things last night. She's very good. I left her to attend to things. She said that she got to bed at two having seen that all the guests were settled.'

'Two in the morning?' Cathy asked in surprise. 'She must be exhausted. Surely, that wasn't expected. Drinks wouldn't normally be served after midnight?'

'It's part of the job, doctor. She stayed up to tidy and make sure the guests were comfortable. No doubt your shifts are just as arduous. In our line of work, we aren't dealing with life-or-death decisions though.'

'I think I'm beyond the night shifts now as a GP but I see what you mean. So, Andrea didn't report anything unusual?'

'She's not in this morning, obviously, but no. Nothing out of the ordinary. I've spoken to her and broken the sad news by telephone. She'll be in this afternoon to speak to the police, of course.'

Cathy nodded. 'Right. Thank you.' She stepped sideways. 'I'll let you get on.'

'You take a particular interest yourself in the matter?' he asked before she could leave.

Cathy's heart quickened. 'Not especially. I didn't know Dr Docherty before. I'm as shocked...'

'But I mean because of your dealings with suspicious death in the past?'

Cathy gaped. 'I've been unfortunate enough to...'

He clapped his hands and smiled, making her flinch. 'Unfortunate? But surely not. The chief inspector will be glad of your help, I think. A mind as sharp as your own will be invaluable. I heard about the little problem at your own practice, then the affair over the gun up at the farm estate. And now, the police ask you to help them again. We count ourselves as fortunate indeed to have you staying with us in such trying circumstances.'

Cathy wasn't sure if he was mocking her. 'If you'll excuse me,' she said, backing away.

Mr Faber bowed, as was his custom.

When she was alone, she realised that her hands were trembling. How had he known about her involvement with the police in the past? Was it the hotel owner's habit to research his guests in such a fashion? All in all, it had been an unsettling encounter.

At the top of the stairs, she turned along the corridor to her room but as she did so, another door opened.

'Oh, Jamie.'

The young man stood in the doorway. His face was haggard. 'I thought I heard a... It doesn't matter. Hello. Are you...?'

'I was just going to freshen up and then I'm going down again. It's been quite a morning, hasn't it?'

'I couldn't face sitting with them all.' His words were impassioned but his body language seemed quite defeated. 'Mr

Faber has been very accommodating. I couldn't share a room with that man any more. Not with anyone.'

'Oh, was this not your original room?'

Jamie nodded across the corridor. 'He's still over there. I moved. I'm glad to be alone. It's better that way. God knows who decided to put me with him anyway.'

'Jamie, are you all right? I realise you and Ryan perhaps haven't seen eye-to-eye and I know Kenneth was quite hard on you yesterday afternoon. I think all of us were uncomfortable with the way he spoke. Duncan certainly had concerns over Kenneth's training techniques. But his death, well I suppose we're all in shock.'

'I suppose I deserved what he said to me. Things don't always come naturally, but I work hard. That's why I am where I am now. It's been a struggle, Cathy. If you must know, it's been a terrible struggle. It's a job I love, but... I want to do it well. Can you understand that?' He looked at her keenly, as if trying to decide. 'Sometimes the pressure to get things right...'

'You told me last night that you've been a community nurse practitioner for some years. I'm sure you're excellent at your job. And you want to improve yourself by coming to these training events. What was it that made you come on the course? That's if you don't mind me asking?'

He seemed to be looking up the corridor past her. Instinctively, she turned and looked over her shoulder. No one was there.

'A work incident. I felt out of my depth. I always swore I'd never let myself feel that way again. This was the first course I could get on. I've been on the waiting list for a year and a half but they prioritise GPs. You're apparently more likely to need the critical incident training.' The final sentence was dripping with cynicism.

Cathy nodded. 'And last night, you went up early to read?'

'I couldn't stomach watching them drinking themselves silly. Especially an instructor. No one seemed to be taking it seriously at all. It was wrong. That's what I thought.'

Cathy nodded. 'You shared a room with Ryan last night but he says you weren't there when he went up?'

He snorted. 'I struggle to sleep. I went for a walk.'

'Had you and Ryan met before the course?'

He looked hard at her. 'Watch him.'

'Excuse me?'

His voice was low and his words earnest. 'Watch him,' he whispered. 'That man isn't what he seems. Poison.'

Cathy was aware once more that he was scanning the corridor behind her and it was all she could do to stop herself from looking behind herself again. 'I don't understand, Jamie.' She shook her head.

But it was clear that the moment had passed. Having bent low to speak with her, he straightened up. 'I'll let you get on, Cathy,' he said in an excessively breezy manner. 'Nice to chat.'

Returning to her room, Cathy closed the door. Leaning back on its cold wooden surface, she sighed. What on earth had Jamie meant about Ryan? Huntington Lodge housed more secrets than even she had imagined.

18

'It's no secret.' Gus laughed, but the sound was forced and the smile didn't reach his eyes.

'Well, why do I feel so bad then?' Mary asked him. Two red patches had formed on her cheekbones. He'd seen it when she was indignant. Over the years, he'd teased her for it, making her even more incensed than before.

'You're being oversensitive. Look, I'm sorry I snapped. You can tell whoever you like. It's just I didn't want the thing to be the focus of their attention. You know what it's like here. As soon as something like that gets out, people are all over it and especially because of who we are.'

Mary nodded. 'I'm sorry, Gus, really I am. I wasn't thinking. It's difficult for me though, you do see that? I'm trying but it is hard.'

He went to her and kissed her cheek. 'Of course, I know. It's been you I've been worrying about all this time, not myself. Listen, it doesn't matter a jot. They'd be bound to find out soon enough. I saw Malcolm on the boat coming back and they all knew I was on the mainland all that morning anyway. I know fine well that with nothing other than poor old Reenie Mathers's passing, there's little else to gossip about.'

Mary looked skyward and moaned. 'Oh but, Gus. It wasn't gossip. Darling, please don't even think that. I needed to talk and I will do more and more. I wish you'd be more open...'

He tutted. There was only so much he could take after all. 'I need to get on.' He felt the sickening guilt of someone who knows they are hurting the person they love the dearest. 'Surgery starts in half an hour and I'm going in past Andrews's on the way.'

She nodded. Her face was pale and her eyes watery.

'We'll talk this evening, Mary. I don't have time for it just now. You make a nice dinner and we'll sit and talk about things then.'

All afternoon he worried. Between his patients, his hands twitched in his lap. Annoyed with himself, he got up and strode up and down the small consulting room. He hated falling out and she was just worried. She had been having nightmares again, that he knew. They'd not spoken of it but the past three nights, he'd had to wake her to spare her the torment. Always the same, even after all these years. Her legs kicking. In the past, she'd explained to him that she had been treading water. And then she'd begin to whimper. It was a pitiful sound and quite childlike. Calling out again and again. Sometimes she'd wake herself up before he managed. The name was always just on her lips, a gasping whisper. 'Becca.'

When they had first married, it had come as a bit of a shock. She'd never mentioned it before despite the hours they'd spent sitting together on the shore or up by her parents' house in the dying sun, the breeze catching and whipping her hair across her face so that she snatched it, flicking the strands from her parched lips. Hours too, she had sat patiently by him as he worked from home, sometimes advising his patients over the telephone and at other times, driving out to their houses. In the beginning, she'd come and sit in the car. Happy to wait for him no matter how long he took. Pleased to be with him for any length of time, not expecting conversation when he returned, just content to be near.

When they had started courting, he had already met her parents professionally. Her father, a gruff lifelong islander and heavy drinker, had taken his hand and shaken it until his arm hurt. Her mother had been shy and deferential. Gus smiled in recollection. In all the ten years that they saw their daughter married to him, Mary's mother never called him Gus, always Dr McAlver. They had been delighted to see their daughter settled with a successful husband but more than that, they were relieved that she'd then have no reason to leave. Perhaps they knew that had she not fallen in love with Gus, she'd have to look for a husband on the mainland. It was what happened and more often than not, people didn't come back. They said that they would, but having seen how comfortable life could be, how fast things were done in civilisation, it was hard to return to the slow pace and the backward thinking of Skeln.

After a meal with her parents one evening and only a year or so into their marriage, he had teased her. Mary's mother had been washing the dishes in the kitchen and her father, pouring a glass of whisky for himself and his son-in-law, although Gus told him it would have to be a small dram as he was always on call.

'Come on then and tell me one thing,' Gus had laughed. They had been goofing around in the kitchen, talking about her sleep-talking and Mary's mother had confessed to finding Mary on the front doorstep as a child having apparently sleepwalked downstairs in the middle of the night and locked herself out.

'Well then?' Mary had giggled, looking up at him, her cheeks flushed and her eyes dancing. 'Tell you what? You're hoping one night to hear me say another man's name so you can act jealous, aren't you, but I won't!'

Gus had flicked her with a tea towel and Mary's mother had shrieked and scolded them.

'I've heard no men mentioned as yet,' he laughed, 'but who in the name of goodness is Becca?'

He knew as soon as the name had left his lips that he'd made a mistake. The whole house fell silent.

'Sorry,' he said. 'Maybe I shouldn't...'

They didn't speak of it again for days and when she finally told him, he wished he hadn't asked.

19

'Where the hell have you been then?'

Cathy smiled at her friend's reaction. Suzalinna had leapt up as soon as the door opened. They were still all gathered in the Islay Suite. Suzalinna had found herself a shady spot in a rather upright armchair at the window. The curtain, no longer tied back, hung in loose velvety folds, the dark green a stark contrast to Suzalinna's red blouse.

'You'd never believe me if I told you,' Cathy said, smiling despite the seriousness of the situation. She nodded at Charles who had raised a hand in greeting. He and Duncan were seated at the far end of the room. Cathy found herself blushing when Duncan looked across at her and she wondered if he was recounting to the rest of them what she had been doing now she was in the police detective's confidence.

Suzalinna raised her eyebrows and looked nonplussed. 'Well?'

'I'm surprised you hadn't heard already. Don't laugh,' Cathy whispered, 'but the chief inspector asked me to sit in on the interviews.'

'What?'

'I know. It felt a bit odd. A bit like being a medical student again, shadowing a senior.'

'I assume he'd heard about your track record?' Suzalinna smirked. 'I did wonder if word would get out about the legendary Dr Moreland.'

Cathy, who had pulled a chair over, lapsed back on it. 'I knew you'd be a pig about it. Well, yes, as it happens, he had. Of course, I have no more right to be listening in than anyone else. God knows how he thinks I'll be able to help. He said he thought my medical mind might be of use.'

'So, what's his take on it then? Does he agree that it was a mismanaged cardiac arrest?'

'No.'

Suzalinna's dark eyes widened as she turned to face her. 'Well, what then?'

'Murder.'

There was a stunned silence. The other group members were out of earshot but even so, Cathy realised that Suzalinna's reaction had drawn attention. From across the room, Ryan sniffed and nodded at them.

'No way,' Suzalinna finally said, covering her mouth.

Cathy nodded. 'He was hoping someone might have confessed to the failed resuscitation by now, but the fact that no one has does look rather suspicious. I mean, who would just leave him there like that if there hadn't been some kind of foul play? It isn't good whatever way you look at it.'

'So, we're all being interviewed as potential suspects and then what?'

'We're to stay put for the time being. He doesn't want people leaving the hotel. I called Chris just now to say I doubt we'll be allowed home tonight. He's on call anyway so he's staying in the hospital rather than coming back to an empty house. Have you spoken to Saj yet?'

95

'I called him earlier. He wanted to come and pick us up but I told him we were stuck waiting to hear. I wonder if he'd be able to find out the post-mortem results when they come in.'

Cathy shrugged. Suzalinna's long-suffering husband, Saj, was a hospital pathology consultant and dealt with routine post-mortems in the area, but anything suspicious would go to the police surgeons. In the past though, Saj had used his connections to find out details ahead of their announcement. 'Better not ask, Suz,' she suggested. 'We don't want to annoy the chief inspector.'

Suzalinna smiled wickedly. 'No, not now that you're best chums. Why are you here anyway if you're helping him?'

Cathy crossed her legs. 'Martha refused to let me stay for her interview. I thought I should sit here and wait. The hotel's crawling with suited men. Detectives, I assume. I met that creepy Mr Faber earlier.' She leaned forward. 'Is it just me, or does he make your skin crawl too?'

Suzalinna giggled. 'I thought he was a bit ingratiating.'

'Toadying? Yes. He has a way of bowing and calling you "doctor".' Cathy laughed. 'I saw Jamie upstairs too. I went to freshen up...'

'Still sticking to his room, is he?'

Cathy nodded. 'He's swapped rooms so he's on his own away from Ryan now. He seems happier with that arrangement but... I got a bit of a funny feeling about him.'

'Oh?'

'Hmm. I wondered if he'd had mental health issues. Paranoia, possibly?'

'Yes, I could see that,' Suzalinna agreed. 'Perhaps it's justified though. Ryan certainly hates his guts, doesn't he? The way he threw him under a bus earlier suggesting that he was prowling around in the dead of night. Of course, the same could be said for Ryan himself though. If Jamie wasn't in his room, Ryan has no one to corroborate that he was there. I didn't much like the way he mentioned it, anyway.'

The two women looked across the room. Ryan had moved now that Martha was being interviewed and was instead sitting with Joan. The young GP was saying something to Joan. He cupped his hand over her ear in a mock whisper and Joan laughed. Charles didn't smile.

'Something a bit strained there too, I think,' Cathy commented. 'I suspect Jamie and Ryan knew one another before the course. I wonder if anyone else knew Ryan also.'

'He seemed very competent during the practicals yesterday. Over the meal he was charming but a bit of a brag, I thought.'

Cathy nodded. 'Undoubtedly that. You didn't see, but when he first walked in the room yesterday morning, Jamie dropped his notes. Kenneth came in then and nothing was said but it was a little odd.'

Suzalinna raised her eyebrows but turned as the door opened, as did the rest of the room. Having allowed Martha back in, the chief inspector stepped forward. 'Dr McKinley?' Joan and Charles got up. 'Our turn to be interrogated,' Charles said, brushing the creases from his trousers. Joan hovered uncertainly. 'I'd rather Joan and I were interviewed together,' he said. 'Our accounts will be much the same so it makes sense.'

The chief inspector looked like he was going to argue but, raising his hands in acceptance, allowed it.

Cathy got up also, wondering if she too would be required but the chief inspector turned to her. 'No, if you don't mind, Dr Moreland. I'll deal with this alone.'

Cathy blushed and sat down once more. It had been he who had asked for her help originally, certainly not her who offered it. Now she felt like a disgraced school girl. Martha made no eye contact with her at all and walked immediately across to Ryan who was standing by the bay window.

'I'm sorry to keep you waiting Dr Bhat and Dr Oliver. I'll be as quick as I can,' the chief inspector said. He led Joan and Charles into the corridor and closed the door once more.

'What did you do wrong?' Suzalinna asked.

'No idea. Maybe Martha said something dreadful. Perhaps I'm under suspicion now,' Cathy hissed. She looked across and saw Ryan touching the other woman's arm.

'Now who sounds paranoid?' Suzalinna asked. 'You and Martha haven't found much common ground, have you?'

Cathy shook her head. 'Not really. I'm not taking it personally. I don't think she likes sharing a room. She was fine when we first met. I suppose she could do the same as Jamie and ask to swap.'

'Or you could join me, darling,' Suzalinna suggested. 'Well, I don't see why not,' she added when Cathy looked at her. 'I know I was your instructor before and we didn't want to show any favouritism, but that's all fallen by the wayside now, hasn't it? What would it matter if you did swap rooms? I think it's the perfect solution if Martha's blowing hot and cold with you.'

'I don't want to be childish,' Cathy said.

Suzalinna tutted. 'I don't think you are. If you don't get on... She seemed nice enough to me over the meal last night. Told me she'd recently taken on a partnership and it sounded as if she was perhaps struggling to find her feet. A conscientious sort. She's an Edinburgh graduate. Been locuming all over the place since passing her college exams. Said she'd even taken a tour of the Highlands and islands before she was tied down with a permanent post and family.'

'That's interesting. You know Joan and Charles are heading to an island off the west coast? I wonder if she locumed there on her travels. They've been advertising the GP position for ages but being so remote, it wasn't an easy fill. Joan called it a last hurrah before they retire. I think Charles was less keen. More of a city GP, I'd say. Used to nurses jumping when he clicks his fingers and probably prefers the convenience of a hospital close by. This course was a prerequisite for them going to Skeln. Pre-hospital care will have to be damn good when the closest hospital is a three-hour boat trip away.'

'What happens if they don't pass? I assume they can't go?'

Cathy nodded. 'I guess so. I said as much to the chief inspector. This course seems to have been of great importance, if not crucial, to some. I had begun to wonder about that. The temptation of sneaking down to the scenario rooms last night when everyone else was drinking or asleep might have been too great for someone. Might a member of the group have decided to make certain of their pass and actually cheat? Was so vital to complete the course that they decided to get an early look at the scenario so they could swat up overnight? I wonder if Kenneth saw them going down the corridor and followed. He, in his drunken state, could have cornered them...'

'What and they panicked and killed him to prevent exposure?'

Cathy sighed. 'It seems unlikely but what else have we got?' She looked around the room once more. 'Horrible to think of any of them in that way, but I suppose we have to face facts. Currently, we're more than likely to be sitting making small talk with a murderer.'

20

'I've heard a rumour,' Ryan said, sidling up to Cathy at lunch. Mr Faber had laid on a buffet in the neighbouring room and the entire group were released by the chief inspector. There was a collective sigh of relief as they left the Islay Suite. The atmosphere had been strained to say the least and despite the traumatic start to their day, everyone agreed that by half past one, they were incredibly hungry.

Cathy was just helping herself to an egg and cress sandwich from the long table when Ryan nudged her elbow. 'Oh?' she asked. 'What rumour is that then?'

'I heard that you were in on things with the police. You've helped them in the past with something or other, have you? Now I think about it, I do seem to recall hearing about your practice and a little misfortune there a couple of years ago. I hadn't linked you to it though. Private detective, are we? I had better watch what I'm saying.'

Cathy felt herself blush. 'It's not something I care to dwell on, to be honest. Anyway, I don't think the police need much assistance, do they? They're obviously going to interview us in turn and wait for the post-mortem to come back.'

'How long will that be, though? You've dealt with this sort of thing before. What do you think?'

Cathy shrugged but before she could answer, Ryan was grinning. 'Who knows what might happen while we wait? You read books about this sort of thing but you never think it'll happen in real life. A murder mystery in a remote hotel. All the guests begin to look at one another in a new and suspicious way. Which one of us did it? Well, Cathy? Who was it that killed Kenneth?'

Cathy ignored the last comment as it was accompanied by a horrible smirk. Ryan, at least, seemed to be enjoying the unfolding drama. 'I suppose the PM might take a day or so. Perhaps less if it's straightforward,' she said. 'At least when we know how he died we'll be able to put this sort of scandalmongering to one side.'

Ryan had piled his plate high with four sandwiches and a sausage roll. He now moved on to the salad. 'What are your thoughts then, Cathy?' he asked, not put off by her serious tone. 'Have you come up with a theory yet? I saw you talking to your friend Suzalinna. Which one of us did it then? Who's top of your list?'

She grimaced. Even in jest, it was hard to stomach. As they moved to a corner of the room, Cathy explained what she and Suzalinna had originally assumed about the failed resuscitation.

Ryan shook his head and with a sandwich in his hand, pointed to the rest of the group lined up at the table still. 'One of them did it deliberately,' he said and grinned. 'Both you and I know it, so why are you beating around the bush and pretending otherwise? Am I chief suspect?' He looked at her playfully, his eyes wide.

'If you were, I would hardly discuss it with you. But you don't have an alibi, do you?'

Ryan was momentarily taken aback. His eyes widened but

almost before she had a chance to register the change, he was grinning again. 'True enough, Cathy. I can only say that you'll have to believe me. I wasn't creeping about the hotel hoping to murder people. You'll just have to take my word on that.'

'At the moment, I don't believe anything until it's proven but I don't want to discuss it anymore.'

He nodded. 'No, even if you do know more than the rest of us having sat in with the police chief, you'd probably better not say anything else.'

She raised her eyebrows.

'You'd be putting yourself at risk, of course,' he explained. 'There's a killer on the loose. We don't want a second murder, now do we, Cathy?'

Cathy stopped mid-bite. The bread stuck to the roof of her mouth. But Ryan was beaming. He'd seen Martha struggling to carry both plate and drinks over and went to help.

'What was he saying to you?' Suzalinna asked, coming across. 'He was grinning like a bloody Cheshire cat.'

'Well essentially, he warned me that I'm likely to be the next victim.'

'What?'

'Oh, he was being facetious but I didn't find it very funny. Perhaps I'd better not dig around too much.'

'Were you planning to? I have to say, I tend to agree. We're in a volatile and very unusual situation here. All of us crammed up in one hotel. We're bound to look at one another now with some distrust. Best leave it to the chief inspector this time, Cathy. I realise you'd probably have the whole thing sorted by tomorrow morning if you were doing the interviews, but I'm a bit rattled. You know I'm not one for getting feelings about things, but sitting in that room next door all morning, made me think. Even before any of this happened, I had a bad feeling.'

'Can you put your finger on why?'

Suzalinna grimaced. 'I suppose it was the practical training yesterday afternoon,' she said. 'Yes, I think that's when I began to feel uneasy. Of course, I told you already that the meal the previous night was awful because Kenneth and Duncan didn't get on, but it was the course participants that worried me more, I think.'

'Who? Can you be more specific?'

'Not really,' Suzalinna admitted. 'Maybe it's what you were saying earlier on, about people knowing one another before coming here.'

'What, Jamie and Ryan?'

'Not just them...'

'Well, who? I was going to ask Ryan about Jamie just now. He's an odd one though. Hard to pin down.'

But Suzalinna was thinking. 'I'm trying to remember who said what.' She frowned in concentration. 'I had all of you in small groups remember, and you rotated around each station? One with me, one with Kenneth and one with Duncan.'

'I was with Jamie,' Cathy began.

'Yes, yes. Don't rush it. Let me think.'

Cathy waited.

'We put Joan and Charles in different groups, didn't we? Kenneth suggested that. He thought she was relying on him too much or was it the other way around?'

Cathy tutted.

'Well, how was I to know someone was going to die the next day? I can't remember everything,' Suzalinna huffed.

'Martha was with Joan, and Charles was with Ryan,' Cathy said. 'I remember Duncan saying that it should have been boy-girl, but Kenneth shot him down and told him not to change it around.'

'That's right.'

'So, which pairing worried you?'

Suzalinna looked up. At the table, Charles was causing a stir over the lack of a certain type of sandwich.

'I wish you wouldn't make such an exhibition of yourself,' his wife said testily.

Suzalinna turned to Cathy, her eyes wide with satisfaction. 'Of course. It was Charles and Ryan. I'm sure they knew one another before they came here. Charles said something to him at the beginning. "Better not start anything up again," he said.'

'Start anything up? What does that mean?'

'I've no idea, Cathy. I don't know if it's of significance, but I didn't like it. It made me feel as if something was wrong. And now that we're speaking about it, he shouldn't have been here at all.'

'Who?'

'Ryan. He was meant to be on the last course but swapped with someone only a week before. Kenneth mentioned it over the meal the previous night. Said something about causing a lot of difficulty with the organisers as they had to dash around and try to fill the space.'

'That can't have been too difficult though,' Cathy said. 'Isn't there a huge waiting list?'

Suzalinna shrugged. 'I don't know but it makes you think though, doesn't it? Did he find out the list of participants for this course and decide to make certain he was present on this intake?'

Cathy ate the remainder of her sandwich in silence. What Suzalinna had said was of concern but something didn't make sense. Jamie, who was still to join them for lunch and presumably chose to stay in his bedroom and starve rather than face the rest of the group, had said something earlier. He had been trying to get on the course for months but this was the first spot they had had. Why then, hadn't he joined the previous group if Ryan had pulled out at the last minute? Had someone been intent on arranging things so that all of these people were in the hotel together at the same time? And if that was so, who had it been? Kenneth? If it had been him, he'd paid the price for it now.

Cathy looked around the room, her eyes finally coming to rest on Duncan. He had been partly responsible for organising the event. He had told the chief inspector as much earlier when he mentioned his difficulty in dealing with Kenneth's emails. Could Duncan be at the heart of things somehow and if so, what had he planned to achieve in gathering this particular group together?

'You've gone quiet, Cath,' Suzalinna said. 'I never like it when you do that.'

Cathy smiled but she felt little pleasure. 'I don't like any of it, Suz. Not one bit.'

21

J oan looked at Cathy and smiled. They were sitting together in the conservatory. The chief inspector had taken Suzalinna through for her interview following lunch. With only Ryan left, he said that the rest might now move freely about the hotel, obviously avoiding the corridor that was marked with police tape. Martha had gone straight up to their room and Cathy, not wanting to be caught in the awkwardness that might occur if she joined her, decided to sit in the conservatory instead until Suzalinna was free. Joan had joined her on one of the low wicker sofas. The light streamed in the windows but Mr Faber had chosen to shade the roof panels with fawn-coloured blinds so it was not overly glaring. The two women sat for some minutes in amicable silence. Cathy watched as the figure of a man walked to the end of the garden. When he turned towards the hotel, she saw it was Duncan.

'Joan, can I ask a bit of an odd question?' she began.

'Your questions can't be any stranger than those the chief inspector just asked me and Charles.' Joan smiled but her eyes were strained. 'What is it, Cathy? It's been quite a day, hasn't it? I thought you were really impressive earlier, by the way. I'd wanted to say before but there never seemed to be the right time. I don't care what the others are saying, I think you were the most clear-headed amongst all of us.'

Cathy was rather taken aback. She stared at Joan. 'What have the others been saying about me? I don't understand?'

'Oh, I shouldn't have said anything.' Joan laughed, still gazing out of the window. 'No, it's female jealousy really. Just after the police asked you to go through. But forget what I said. It was meant to be a compliment, Cathy. The way you handled yourself when we found that poor man lying there dead was quite something. The rest of us were faffing around panicking and you, well, you were quite calm. Amazing really, considering what we'd just discovered.'

'Right.' Cathy swallowed, not sure quite how to proceed with this new information. The only 'female' who could have said anything was Martha. Exactly what had the other woman said about her?

'Anyway,' Joan said, batting a fly away, 'what was it you wanted to ask?'

Cathy shook her head slightly, trying to collect her thoughts. 'It was simply about everyone on the course. I got the feeling some people might have known one another from before...'

Joan's eyes widened and Cathy knew at once that she had been right.

'I thought Charles and Ryan perhaps...?' she began.

Joan's hands fluttered and she fidgeted with her blouse collar. 'Years ago. Not seen him in years,' she said.

Cathy didn't speak.

'I didn't know him, of course,' Joan said, now quite composed. She smiled thinly, perhaps recognising that her reaction gave her away. 'It's no secret really. I'd been doing family planning clinics up until ten years back. That was when I joined Charles' practice full-time. Charles used to be a trainer, you see?'

'Oh, but no longer?'

'No. Too old and worn down with the daily grind now, but he did enjoy it for a time. Some of these trainees could be quite difficult though.' She laughed nervously. 'He had one lad who could barely speak English once; another had made countless mistakes. One was struck off a couple of years after Charles taught him. I suppose you never know what you're going to end up with and the faculty don't seem to care. They just want to get them through the training and qualified. Perhaps it's all changed now. Guidelines and hoops to jump through. Charles had enough of it though. I said at the time, there's no point in being a trainer if you've lost enthusiasm yourself.'

Cathy nodded.

'Anyway,' Joan said, swallowing. 'Ryan must have been one of the early ones. I never met him, as I say. He was good, so Charles said. Well, he knew his stuff anyway and he's clearly done fine for himself. He was telling me earlier that he's been twelve years in practice now, not that he's counting.' She laughed again but Cathy wasn't convinced. 'Yes. Very competent and good. We've seen that already with his practical abilities yesterday. No doubt he would have passed the assessments here without an issue if they had gone ahead. I wonder what will happen now...'

'You mean for the course? I assume after this business is cleared up, they will rearrange the entire training event. Call everyone back in a month or two.'

'Oh, but Charles and I take up our position on Skeln in a matter of weeks. We must get our certificates first before they allow us to go.'

'Maybe Suzalinna can help. I'm not sure.'

'Yes, I'll speak to her. Surely there's no real need for us to do the entire course again. She'll sign something I expect and that'll allow us to go. Charles might have a word instead of me. He's very persuasive.'

'It's funny Charles and Ryan having known one another from before, isn't it?' Cathy said, returning to the original topic.

Joan hunched her shoulders. 'Not so very unusual. We're all Scottish GPs and might well meet at these kinds of events over the years, I suppose.'

'Not all GPs. You're forgetting one of us is a nurse practitioner.'

'Jamie? Yes, well you know what I mean. He seems like a fish out of water though. Charles said he reminded him of someone the other evening. Funnily enough, now that we're talking about it, he said he was like one of his old trainees.'

'Oh?'

Joan nodded. 'He was being silly of course. Charles has a bit of a superiority thing going on. Rubs people up the wrong way often. Nurse practitioners have a new role to play and Charles doesn't adapt well to change. His view is that nurses have their job to do and we have ours. When you start muddying the water with these highly trained practitioners, that's when the trouble starts. People don't know where they stand.'

Cathy raised her eyebrows. 'It's a positive development as far as I can see.'

'Yes, well you're young and flexible. Charles is retiring in a few years and can't see it that way. Skeln will suit him well. It's thirty years behind the times so he'll fit in perfectly.'

Cathy looked out again at the garden. On the path now stood another figure. It was a man, tall and slender. Jamie approached Duncan and the two men stood together for some time.

'He's finally made it downstairs,' Joan commented, nodding at Jamie. 'Well, I suppose I had better track down that husband of mine. If he's to speak with Dr Bhat about our certificates, he'd be better doing it sooner rather than later. I'll get him to have a word as soon as she finishes with the chief inspector perhaps. But where he's got to, I don't know.'

'Maybe the same place as this morning...'

Joan looked sharply at her. 'He was in the garden first thing. Just taking a stroll. It's easy to lose track of time, and how was he to know someone was going to be found dead and he'd be asked where he was?'

Cathy nodded. 'No, I wasn't meaning to be funny really. It was just curious that it was only the women who found poor Kenneth, that's all. I don't think the police care where he was in the morning. After all, it was last night when Kenneth died.'

The older woman got up and steadied herself on the arm of the chair. 'Yes, well I'd better find him now.'

'Joan, when Charles said that Jamie reminded him of one of his trainees, did he say which one?'

Joan looked out the window. Jamie and Duncan appeared to be deep in conversation. Jamie stood with his head bowed slightly beside the shorter man.

Joan seemed to almost forcibly draw her attention back to Cathy. When she spoke it was with a meditative tone. 'It was the one who was struck off, now you ask.' She shrugged seeing Cathy's surprise. 'It's what he said anyway. If you knew Charles, you'd understand. He was probably being an old fool. I don't listen to half the things he says, Cathy. If I did, I'd have divorced or killed him by now.'

22

When Suzalinna emerged from her interview with the chief inspector, she hunted for Cathy, only to find her still sitting in the conservatory. Joan had long since left and she sat with only her thoughts for company.

'All alone?' Suzalinna asked, her heels clicking on the flagstone floor. 'I had wondered if you'd gone up to the room with a headache; or is Martha there?'

Cathy rolled her eyes. 'My head's fine but, yes, I'm steering well clear of Martha for now especially as I've just heard from Joan that she's been bad-mouthing me.'

'Oh?'

But Cathy shook her head. 'It doesn't matter. Tell me how you got on. Did Chief Inspector Forbes pump you for info? Is he any nearer to working it out?'

Suzalinna sat down heavily beside her and sighed. 'Well, he did quiz me a bit. He wanted to know what Kenneth said to me on the first night. You know, before the rest of you arrived? I assume Duncan's been blabbing to him.'

Cathy turned to face her. 'I meant to ask you about that. You keep brushing over it, but when I sat in on Duncan's interview, he did mention Kenneth saying something spiteful to you. He went on to hint that it put you in the frame as much as anyone else. Not hugely tactful, I must say but I think he was a little overwrought when he was answering the chief inspector and probably wanted to take the pressure off himself a little. Anyway, what was it all about? What did Kenneth say that first night?'

'It was something and nothing really.'

Cathy waited with her eyebrows raised.

Suzalinna glanced at her and giggled. 'Not the look, Cathy! You know I'm afraid of you when you look like that. Okay, I admit it. I killed him! I'm the murderer!'

Cathy snorted. 'Idiot. Well, what did Kenneth say to upset you?'

Suzalinna sighed, her eyes flitted across the garden lawn and the flowering borders. 'He'd heard about Roderick.'

They sat in silence for some moments, the light-hearted atmosphere forgotten. Then Cathy finally spoke. 'Suz–'

'Yes,' Suzalinna said, deliberately interrupting. 'It was a shock to have it brought up. Kenneth had done his digging. I've no idea how he got hold of it. It's five years now and no one speaks about it anymore. All but forgotten.'

The words were off-hand but Cathy knew only too well that it still played on her friend's mind a good deal.

'What did Kenneth say?'

Suzalinna rubbed her nose with her finger. 'It started, I seem to remember, with one of his boastful tales. Kenneth began his career in A&E himself, as you might imagine. That was before he was lured away by the excitement of helicopters. Anyway, that evening, he told some story about a medical student fainting during a messy arrest when he was a senior registrar in A&E.'

Cathy nodded.

'Well, I suppose I was bored by that point and didn't respond in the right way. You know I can be a bit of a pig when I'm fed up? Well, perhaps I didn't laugh in the right place or bolster his ego enough. It had been going on all night, you know? He'd been bragging non-stop and Duncan and I had just to sit and listen to it while he got more and more drunk. He was sitting opposite me and swilled his whisky around his glass. He looked me straight in the eye and said, in front of Duncan remember: "Of course, your track record isn't so rosy with students is it, Dr Bhat?"'

Cathy sucked in her breath. 'How did you react?'

'Well, I felt sick. I didn't know if he knew. He laughed and slugged down his whisky. All the while, my mind was going like crazy. So, he elbowed Duncan, and I can still recall his smug face now, Cathy. "A suicide after a placement in your own department," he said. "Bet that took a bit of explaining afterwards. Not a reflection on your teaching, I hope!"'

Her face was white as she said this and Cathy reached out and touched her friend's arm. 'Oh, Suz, I'm sorry, and when you're trying to forget about it all.'

Suzalinna sniffed but her mouth was set firm. 'Oh, I'm over it, Cath, don't worry about me. I was cleared of any wrongdoing at the time. Poor Roderick had a moderate personality disorder. He was a fragile individual and any event might have tipped him. Medicine was a bad career choice for someone so unstable. But, of course, anyone would feel terrible in my position.'

Cathy looked at her. The words were spoken without expression but she knew that Suzalinna still blamed herself for the young medical student's death no matter how forcefully she denied it. 'Not nice to have that dragged up again,' she said quietly.

'No,' Suzalinna agreed. 'No, it wasn't nice at all, Cathy.'

'So, I assume you told the chief inspector? What did he have to say?'

'He jotted it all down and I'm sure he'll look into it. Asked me half a dozen follow-up questions. I could tell exactly what he was thinking.'

'What?'

'That I murdered Kenneth to keep his mouth shut, of course.'

'Don't be ridiculous.'

'It's what Duncan obviously thought if he mentioned it. Goodness knows what they're all saying now.' Suzalinna gestured wildly behind her to the door.

'Well, if it was so easy to discover and if Duncan now knows about it also, what motive would you have for killing Kenneth then?' Cathy asked. 'You see what I mean, don't you? If your motive was to prevent him from telling everyone, and yet, in the same breath, you admit that everyone might easily find out through Duncan, or conceivably for themselves if they really wanted to dig for any dirt on you, well, it means your motive doesn't stand up.'

Suzalinna sighed but didn't look at Cathy.

'Well, you do see that, don't you?' Cathy persisted. 'And anyway, the chief inspector isn't a fool. He's not going to fall for any of that kind of wishy-washy reasoning. He wants hard facts and a real reason to kill, not some tragic misfortune from earlier in your career. As you said yourself, you were exonerated of any blame at the time so what would any of it matter?'

Suzalinna shook her head, her eyes still looked out into the middle distance.

'It does tell us something about Kenneth as an individual though,' Cathy said after a moment's silence.

'Oh, what's that? That he was an absolute idiot?'

'That, obviously, but no, I'm just thinking that it tells us a bit about his personality and maybe even his plans for the emergency course.'

Suzalinna turned to face her.

'Well,' Cathy said. 'What kind of a man does that? Why research your fellow instructors? He was looking to gain the upper hand for some reason of his own. It does beg the question: if he'd examined your past, had he done the same for Duncan?'

Suzalinna swallowed. 'Not just that, but I suppose we should extend that to the rest of them.'

'Yes,' Cathy agreed. 'I've no idea what he was up to, but if he wanted to cause discomfort for one of the course participants, he was in a position to easily do so. Did Kenneth have a quiet word with one of them during the last evening? Did he threaten to expose someone? Maybe it was old-fashioned blackmail for money. Maybe it was out of devilment?'

'Well, if he did, he paid the price for it.'

'Now we need to find out what he knew though, Suz, and if we manage to do that, we'll find who killed him.'

'I thought we'd agreed to leave it to the chief inspector.'

Cathy looked gravely at her friend. 'I find myself a little distrustful now of the chief inspector. I suspect that he's already been swayed by something Martha's said about me, hence why I'm no longer invited into his confidence. I've no idea what Martha said but now that you've been dragged into it, I feel that we'd be foolish to sit here and wait.'

'Like sitting ducks?'

'Either for the chief inspector to come to the wrong conclusion or for one of us to end up in trouble.'

'You take what Ryan said seriously? You think you might be a target now because everyone assumes you're in on things with the police?'

Cathy nodded. 'Yes. I made light of it before but I think, come this evening when the lights go out, I'll be taking the threat incredibly seriously.'

23

He left the upstairs landing light on. It wasn't mentioned but he knew he should. Years ago, she'd explained how threatening the dark was and how frightened she felt with nothing to gauge her whereabouts. Now, it was a silent understanding. In times of difficulty, he knew the nightmares would return. They always did.

They hadn't spoken about it since the letter had arrived. Gus had gone about his duties, more painstakingly and with perhaps more nostalgia. Every consultation would now have to be imprinted into his memory. He'd been doing it more and more since he realised he was dying. That was another thing they hadn't spoken about. She knew. They had both known long before it was confirmed on the mainland over a year ago. Now the appointments were to check the progress of the disease but they were long past stopping it.

He had gone alone to that initial appointment. Of course, he had to. Mary would stay to take any emergency calls for him, to redirect any if necessary or to advise the less urgent ones that he'd be home that afternoon. On the whole, the islanders were understanding. At times demanding, but when it came to it, they understood. He'd given his life to the island and they knew it.

He cast his mind back to that day when he had been told that the cancer had taken hold. When he had returned, Mary had been waiting. She'd seen the ferry from the upstairs window and had walked down to the jetty to meet him, her cotton dress catching in the wind so that she had to press the skirt down with her hands. Surely in her heart, she had known. He smiled at her as the boat began to dock. Its engines roared, forcing water backwards to slow the approach and then, as metal touched stone, the crushing groan.

Gus wondered if she preferred to hear it outside in the open air. Maybe he was being fanciful but perhaps she found the thunder of the sea and the salt on her lips a comfort. They had been her companions for so long after all.

They had walked back towards the house arm-in-arm. Gus had nodded to the Lochty twins who ran past the other way and Mary told him that there had only been three calls all morning and none of them were urgent. Her hand was tight on his sleeve. He felt her chest touching his elbow with every step.

'So,' he said, letting the word escape.

'So.'

They stood at the crest of the hill having passed the end of the harbour and the line of terraced fisherman's cottages that took the full force of the elements on a stormy day.

Their house, the one they had moved into as soon as they were married, was another hundred yards on. The road that led to it had a further four houses but these were spaced apart and each set back off the track. This was the more habitable side to the island and yet it still felt as if they were quite alone. It was how they preferred it. Their house enjoyed an almost private view of the beach, a small pebbled and sandy strip that was often covered by black and green seaweed, crisp underfoot in places and slick and slippery in others. The rocks that sheltered the cove were sharp and rugged. Lichen grew on the larger boulders nearer the road and if you clambered down over the rutted seagrasses and silverweed, its small yellow flowers peeping through grey leaves, you could stand sheltered on the sea ravaged shore.

'Just as we thought, Mary.'

The sea raced in, its turquoise and navy rose and then landed, scampering up the beach in froth and spume.

'Ah, yes. And now?'

He found himself scanning the waves, following their rise and fall, far into the distance. On a fine day, the mainland was almost visible but not today. It was simply a haze of grey where sea met sky.

'Too far on. We discussed some things to slow the progress.'

'Gus...'

She didn't need to look at him, nor he at her. Her hand shifted on his arm.

It was the thing she had begged of him and he had promised her time and again throughout their marriage although, of course, both had known he had no control over the situation. Gus wondered if he should apologise but the word was empty and she knew without him speaking anyway.

He thought about it a lot after that day. When she slept fitfully next to him, he often lay awake wondering how she'd cope.

'Promise?' she had giggled not long after they'd married. 'Never, never leave me, Gus. You won't ever, will you?'

He had kissed her back then, pressing his lips to hers and closing his eyes tight, inhaling the sun-kissed peach of her skin. But it hadn't been enough. Over the years, she had asked him the same. Time and again, the same question. Now he knew why, of course. It was little wonder after what had happened at

Sandeels bay. That dreadful morning seemed to have shaped Mary's entire life. It had changed her forever. After all these years, most of the island had surely forgotten but for her, even the suggestion that it had been anything but an accident haunted her. And sometimes now, when he heard Becca's name whimpered in the darkness, he also heard the word 'murder'.

24

'It *was* murder then,' Ryan said loudly. 'That's why we need to be watched.'

The chief inspector wasn't amused. Having interviewed the entire group, he had asked for them to stay in the hotel that night and promised that there would be a police presence. 'I've said already, Dr Oliver, we're not ready to confirm anything of the sort. All I ask is for a little co-operation while we await the post-mortem results. That should, with any luck, be tomorrow morning.'

'I feel like we're all suspects,' Joan said but the chief inspector shook his head once more.

'You have all travelled from afar to get to the course. Really, the last thing I need is to be calling up each regional division if I require the answers to further questions. Please bear with me just now. We'll be in a better position tomorrow.'

'I don't mind a bit,' Ryan said. 'I was planning on staying the night following the course anyway. I'd already spoken to the hotel manager to tell him.'

Cathy wondered what reason Ryan had to stick around. But then, there were still so many questions that hung around the young medic. So far, she had established that he had been Charles's registrar trainee. Joan said that he had been a good one. Why then had Charles looked so perturbed seeing him? And then there was Jamie. 'Watch that one,' he had said to Cathy earlier. Was it paranoia or was Jamie genuinely afraid of Ryan, and how might their paths have crossed?

'Have you told her yet?' Suzalinna hissed.

The chief inspector had closed the door leaving them to talk amongst themselves.

'You mean Martha? About swapping rooms? I doubt she'll care,' Cathy said, looking across at the other woman. 'She didn't want to share in the first place and she's been charmed by Ryan all afternoon, she'll hardly notice.'

They had already discussed that evening's sleeping arrangements. Cathy, feeling increasingly edgy, had agreed with Suzalinna. It made sense. Martha wouldn't miss her and what could be more natural than sharing with her old friend? Suzalinna had already made it quite clear that she wasn't allowing Cathy out of her sight that night after hearing Ryan's chilling warning.

'Even if she did think it rude, I should think she half expects it. Now I'm not your supervisor anymore, why not bunk in with your old medical school chum?'

'I hope it doesn't look like I'm snubbing her.'

'Who cares? You said yourself that she was bad-mouthing you. I wonder what she said. Let her have the room to herself. I told you before, I want to keep an eye on you now.'

'Because I'm the next potential victim?'

'Well not quite, darling. Hopefully, there will only be one death. But you know Chris wouldn't forgive me if I didn't look after you. Have you phoned him again to say we're staying on?'

'I bleeped him earlier.'

'Saj is having kittens about all of this.' Suzalinna laughed.

'He thought we were safely tucked away in a swanky hotel with no chance of getting involved in anything sinister. You know it is a little odd that these things keep happening to us, don't you think? Saj is going to ban me from kicking about with you if this happens every time we go for a jaunt.'

'Poor Saj,' Cathy agreed. 'Hopefully, by tomorrow we'll get home.'

'I did ask him if he could find anything out from the police surgeons but he said it was too awkward. I suppose it would look a bit cheeky one of the hospital pathologists ringing up and trying to get insider information before the police even had it.'

'Did I hear the words: "insider information"?'

Cathy started but Suzalinna showed no sign of upset and smiled coolly at Ryan who had sauntered over with Martha in tow.

'Perhaps you did,' Suzalinna said and turned her attention to Martha. 'And how do you take the chief inspector's announcement then?'

Martha had been holding a plastic cup from the water fountain and Cathy heard the pliable material crunch in her hand. 'I'm not happy, obviously but we have to do what the police say. I'll co-operate with whatever they tell us to do.'

'Quite,' Suzalinna said. 'This evening will be difficult but we have to do what we have to do.'

Cathy, who had been silent up until now, smiled. 'Martha, I don't suppose you saw anything odd last night? I hear you went out for some fresh air at one point and I wondered if anyone else was in the hotel lobby?'

'I don't know what you mean,' Martha said. Her eyes widened and she glanced at Ryan.

'Well, the hotel is reserved for our group only, I realise that, but it's not as if it's a locked building. People can come and go. I just wondered if you might have seen anything out of the ordinary?'

'A stranger?' Martha asked as if the idea hadn't occurred to her.

'Perhaps...'

Martha looked around her. Other conversation in the room seemed to have dried up, and all eyes were on her. She licked her bottom lip and seemed to be considering what to say. But before she could answer, Ryan laughed and patted her on the back.

'Poor Martha. Put you on the spot, hasn't she?' He turned back to Cathy. The teasing quality to his eyes was no longer present. 'I suppose she's answered enough questions today already, just like the rest of us. It would be a shame to get in the way of the police investigation by muddling up people's accounts of last night. I realise only too well what you're trying to do but really, I think it would be foolish to start anything of that sort here.'

Cathy was quite aware of the threat in his voice. When she later spoke with Suzalinna up in their room, she too agreed that there had been a hint of menace to his words. But what surprised Cathy more that late afternoon was Charles's reaction. He had overheard the conversation, as had the rest of the room, and he came across, standing pointedly, with his back to Ryan.

'Cathy, I'd like to speak with you in private later, if I may? I've heard about your reputation. If it means clearing up this mess quicker, both Joan and I would be happy to answer any of your questions.'

25

The meal that night was even more awful than the previous. The group were bound by a horrible but unmistakable unity but not one of them was beyond suspicion. Cathy wondered if her fellow diners were wondering which one of them was guilty. No one bothered to continue in the pretence that the death might have been accidental. They were beyond that now. And that left only one alternative. Admittedly, what she had said earlier had been true though. The hotel wasn't locked and anyone might come and go up until midnight when, Cathy had discovered discreetly from Andrea, the front doors were locked. Still, she thought, with the bustle of yesterday evening, particularly after Mr Faber had left the younger member of staff to see to the drinks on her own, might Andrea have failed to adhere to protocol? Besides that, there were any number of fire doors and then there was the conservatory that she had sat in also. The large building might well offer an assailant easy access.

But whatever way Cathy looked at it, and however much she wished it not to be someone at the dinner table, she still couldn't convince herself that a stranger had killed Kenneth. Stories of psychotic madmen opportunistically murdering people were outdated nonsense. The majority of murders were committed by someone who knew their victim. Cathy looked around the table of faces. Who had known Kenneth best?

Beside her, Jamie dissected his beef in silence, his knife intermittently squealing on the plate surface. The nurse practitioner had all but given up any attempt at integration and had only come downstairs to appease Mr Faber, who had, it seemed, gone up in person to ask for his presence at dinner. Cathy supposed that making special meal orders for individual rooms would have been a big ask given how hectic the day had been already for the hotel. And although Cathy had taken a bit of a dislike to the hotel owner, she saw the strain of the past day weighed heavily on him.

He had tactfully decided to serve them their meal in a different room from the previous day and they had, without needing to vocalise it, seated themselves in different positions, not wanting to recreate the actions of the night before. Still, Cathy found herself looking around the table and feeling guilty. They were sitting down to a jolly good feed and one of them had died less than twenty-four hours before. It seemed insincere and rather horrible, but as Suzalinna had pointed out earlier, they really must eat and if it so happened that the food was good, well, who were they to complain?

Throughout the meal, Mr Faber, dressed immaculately as always, hovered in the background overseeing his staff. But his face looked pained and Cathy judged from the dark shadows beneath his eyes that he hadn't slept well the previous night even before the dreadful discovery had been made. Andrea also looked worried and uncertain. Cathy knew that a good deal of the police questions might rest on her evidence. She had been the only sober person downstairs and her account might well be the most accurate.

To the right of Jamie, Joan was talking with Martha about their planned adventure and speculating about island life as a doctor. Cathy overheard Martha telling the older GP that she had done some locum work on the inner Hebridean islands not long after finishing her training.

'A funny way of life and not for me,' she had admitted.

An odd coincidence that she had worked there, but perhaps there had been too many of those in the last day or so for it to be simply that. So many invisible threads seemed to link the group. Cathy knew that she must speak to Martha in private that evening if she got the chance. She felt sure that Ryan had stopped the other woman just as she was going to tell her something when they had spoken earlier. As she watched Martha nodding and smiling with Joan, she wondered if she might have seen the person responsible for Kenneth's death behaving suspiciously in the hotel lobby. She said she had been going to get some fresh air. Cathy didn't believe her but had she spotted one of the course participants outside the scenario rooms while the rest continued to drink following the previous night's meal? At the time, it would have meant nothing to her, but had she since recalled the oddity and wondered?

But as it turned out, it proved difficult to pin Martha down. If Cathy was honest, it felt as if the other woman was deliberately avoiding her that evening. Before dinner, Cathy had mentioned swapping rooms that night but Martha hadn't seemed particularly surprised.

'Sure,' she had said. 'Whatever suits you best.'

If Cathy was pushed, she might have said that there was a flash of triumph in Martha's expression but it was so fleeting, it was gone before she was sure.

Mr Faber had been circling the room with a drinks tray and had overheard them discussing the new room arrangements.

'I hope that's all right?' Cathy asked him. 'I suppose I should have mentioned it to you. Suzalinna and I were at medical school together. We thought it made sense. You won't need to make up a new bed or anything so hopefully, it's not an issue.'

Ever professional, the hotel owner flashed his teeth disarmingly and nodded. 'Not at all. Not at all. I can see how it might be for you and nice for the ladies to have their little chats. I imagine you'll be talking the case through together.' But when Cathy went to speak, he touched his lips. 'Oh, but I've said too much.' He smiled and left her.

When the dessert was brought out to them, things seemed less tense than they had at first been, although next to her, Cathy rather wished that Jamie had remained monosyllabic. Across the table, Charles was wondering loudly who would be footing the hotel bill as the group had essentially been forced to stay on an extra night that they otherwise might not.

'Not to mention the food and drink,' Charles said. 'Costing us a bloody fortune to stay on when none of us wanted to be here longer than we had to.'

Joan nudged him. 'Stop making a fuss, Charles, for goodness' sake. It'll sort itself out without you interfering.'

Beside her, Suzalinna shifted in her seat. She had told Cathy about the awkwardness that afternoon when Joan asked about the course certification. It sounded very much like she and Charles were in a desperate state. If they didn't have the course signed off, they couldn't go to Skeln. There was a start date that for some reason couldn't be changed. Cathy found it a little difficult to believe this was true and she said so to her friend, but Suzalinna had shrugged.

Apparently, Joan had been on the verge of tears when she had explained that it was a matter for the department to look into. But Suzalinna was an instructor and a new one at that. She had no say over such things. Joan had given up trying to persuade her but before dinner, Cathy had spotted Charles approaching her friend with a rueful smile, clearly trying to change her mind too. He had been told the same as his wife it seemed and sat sulkily until the starters came.

'No, I want to know, Joan,' he insisted now, putting his glass down so hard that the red wine sloshed dangerously high up the side. 'Here we are trying to better ourselves and we get drawn into this mess. I don't think much of the bloody department so far and this tops it all.'

'Drink was always the responsibility of each course participant,' Duncan said curtly. 'I think it was in the information emailed to you right at the start, Charles.'

Jamie put down his dessert spoon and cleared his throat. 'Not quite true,' he said, looking at Duncan. 'I read the information carefully.'

The room was silent and all eyes turned to look at him.

He pushed his glasses up the bridge of his nose, as seemed to be his habit and glared around the table. 'We paid a fixed price for the course. Accommodation and meal on the first night were included. Obviously, if people ordered food or drinks on top of the allotted glass of wine last night, I'm sure they will be expected to pay.'

'And I thought we were just splitting the bill like old friends,' Ryan said languidly. He picked up his half-full wine glass and drank the contents in one quaff. Then, placing it carefully down on the table, he smiled nastily at Jamie.

Jamie looked back defiantly. 'I've already paid my share. I didn't stay up drinking whisky all last night. Nor did I want to stay here this evening. If it hadn't been for the police forcing us, I'd have gone elsewhere.'

Ryan chuckled as if it was the funniest thing he had heard that evening. 'No, you didn't stay up drinking with us, did you?' He pointed a finger at Jamie. 'I wonder though, what you were up to instead...'

A deep crimson crept up Jamie's neck. Cathy thought that his only possible response would be to storm out but Ryan still wasn't done.

'I think you're splitting hairs, anyway,' Ryan said. 'What does it matter really? We can all surely afford to pay a couple of quid. I know some of us are better off than others, of course... As long as the hotel get their money, I'm happy to split the remainder equally, that's if–'

'We'll discuss it later,' Duncan interrupted. 'No doubt the department will have a contingency fund for issues. Don't concern yourself, Jamie, or anyone else. I realise some of us have hardly had a drop of alcohol. It would seem unfair if they had to foot the bill for the rest. I'll get on the phone with the department again tomorrow. Another thing to sort out,' he said to himself.

'I wasn't concerning myself,' Jamie said looking at his plate. 'I'm just stating a fact. I won't be paying for other people's overindulgence.'

'So, you've spoken to the department already, Duncan?' Charles asked. 'Sorry, it was just you said: "again". Did you manage to get through to them about the course in the end? Joan and I are distressed about what has happened here. Of course, we all are. But if there was a way that we could have the course completed? If we could be signed off as competent? I know for some of us, this was probably just a jolly, but others are relying on the certification. Joan's and my circumstances are rather unique as I mentioned to you already earlier in the day...'

Duncan laid his fork and knife down on his plate. 'I wasn't sure if everyone felt the same. I would have spoken with you in private, Charles. Yes, as it happens, I did speak to the department. I had to let them know what was going on anyway and I believe the police have spoken with the powers-that-be about Kenneth's interactions in setting up the event.' He sighed.

'It's all a little distasteful to talk about it but there are rules, Charles. In theory, the situation has always been that if a course participant leaves the event early, they then have no reimbursement from the department for their course fees and obviously, their certification is null and void even if they have performed part, but not all of the course and assessment.'

Charles was shaking his head. 'I don't quite see...'

'No, well it seems quite unreasonable to me given the circumstances, but they say that as the course is still, in effect, possible to complete while we are all here, we can, in theory, finish teaching and assessing you. I'll be honest. It seems to me that they are trying to get out of refunding your original fees. I feel a little uncomfortable even talking about it, let alone teaching you again. But, the fact of the matter is that if you do want to do the course again at a later date, I think you'd be asked to pay all over again.'

Someone kicked the table and the cutlery jangled.

It was Martha who spoke. 'But they can't honestly suggest that we continue, given what happened today? A man died. One of their instructors. Don't they have any feelings? How could we all sit down nicely in the Islay Suite and listen to lectures tomorrow? The very thought of it is absurd.'

'No, I'm not happy about it, Martha, hence why I hadn't said anything before. I don't want to teach or assess any of you. It's utterly inappropriate now, given what we've all been through. I find the suggestion appalling,' Duncan said. 'We need to co-operate with the police so that this dreadful mess can be cleared up as quickly as possible, certainly not worry about assessments and certification now.'

'What about you, Dr Bhat?' Charles asked, turning to Suzalinna. His voice was calm and slightly ingratiating. Cathy found herself inwardly recoiling.

'This is the first I've heard about it,' Suzalinna said. 'Duncan,

I'd like to have a word if I may later? It is certainly something I feel very uncomfortable discussing just now.'

After that, the conversation moved on to safer topics. However, Cathy was in no doubt that Charles wouldn't let the matter drop. No one stayed up after the meal but instead, returned to their rooms with muted goodnights expressed. After all, it seemed unlikely that any of them would sleep particularly well.

26

'Well?' Cathy asked when the door was finally shut. 'What a night.' She had nipped along to the room she had been sharing with Martha and collected her bag. Now, she placed it on the one unruffled bed by the door. It was a twin room, almost identical to the one she had slept in the previous night. Suzalinna had chosen the bed nearest the window and had, in typical fashion, scattered her belongings apparently at random. On the bed that Cathy planned to sleep in, Suzalinna had left a hairdryer and straighteners.

'The whole thing's horrid, isn't it?' Suzalinna agreed, walking through to the bathroom and unzipping her skirt. 'What did you make of Charles?'

'The same as you, I expect. Very persistent. What can be so urgent about getting to Skeln? I know their contract must have a start date, but surely there would be some leeway for extenuating circumstances.'

'I've no idea what it's all about. I'll need to talk to Duncan about it in the morning. The suggestion that we assess you now, after finding Kenneth dead in that room...'

'No, it would be horrible. Charles will just have to accept it.'

'I don't think he and Joan are the only ones though,' Suzalinna said, poking her head around the bathroom door again.

'Oh?' Cathy had begun to unzip her bag and she paused.

'Jamie,' Suzalinna said and rolled her eyes. 'He came and had a word with me just before the meal. He was wondering if we could give certificates out having seen them in practice already.'

Cathy snorted. 'Well, he'd fail if you went by how he performed yesterday. What a ridiculous suggestion.'

Suzalinna was trying to pull an elasticated hairband from her ponytail but it had become tangled. She grimaced as she tugged. 'Yes, darling, I agree, but it does make you think, doesn't it?'

'When I spoke to him in the corridor, he said he had been trying to get on this course for a while. I think he had a chip on his shoulder way back because of that. He had been told that they preferred to offer participant spots to doctors rather than nurse practitioners as they were more likely to need and use the resuscitation training.'

'Well, it was important to him for some reason. I think he'd jump at the chance to finish the course despite what's happened here. They're a cold-hearted bunch, aren't they?'

'Not Martha though,' Cathy said, shaking her head. 'You heard how she reacted. But then I don't trust her much either. She's a bit of a paradox. I told you before she had said something about me to Joan. I don't know what it was but it wasn't complimentary. Then, after she speaks in private with the chief inspector, he wants nothing more to do with me. At the start, he wanted my advice. Now, he won't look at me. It must have been something she said. The other thing I wonder is what she was doing downstairs last night. But then Jamie, and Ryan for that matter, are still unaccounted for too. You'd have thought one of them might have bumped into another while they were creeping about the place.'

Suzalinna sighed. 'They are an odd collection of characters. I wouldn't worry too much about what the bloody chief inspector thinks of you though. Why should you help him anyway? He was putting you in an awkward position asking at all, especially in front of everyone. Even Ryan pointed that out, albeit in a nasty way. It might put you in danger if there is some crazy lunatic on the prowl.' She grinned at Cathy. 'Darling, do you mind if I have a quick shower? I know it's gone eleven but I'm all sticky and I won't sleep.'

Cathy nodded absently. 'Whatever, Suz, go ahead.'

She began to unpack her bag, looking for the pyjamas she had folded carefully earlier. As she pulled her toiletry bag out first, it dropped to the floor. Cathy tutted and bent to pick up the contents. She hadn't zipped it properly and was suddenly reminded of the same thing happening earlier with Martha's bag. Cathy wondered why the other woman had been so sharp with her. It had been as if she thought Cathy was rooting through her things. Did she have something so private that it had to be hidden? Cathy decided that the following morning she'd talk with Martha. There was so much tension between them and she wanted to clear it.

Her toothpaste and hairbrush had rolled onto the floor under the bed covers that hung over the edge. She retrieved the last of her toiletries and was about to straighten up when her finger touched something. Cathy lifted the covers properly now and peered under the bed frame. On the floor, Cathy saw a folded piece of paper. On her hands and knees, she reached to retrieve it. In the bathroom, she could hear Suzalinna humming a tune to herself.

'Just move my stuff, Cath,' Suzalinna called through. 'You know what I'm like, I like to spread out.'

'I don't know why you brought all this anyway,' Cathy said distractedly, now holding the scrap of paper. She turned it over. Suzalinna's name was written in black ink on one side but it had been folded lightly in two. Without thinking, Cathy unfolded it and read the scrawled message.

How do you sleep at night after what you did? BITCH. The last word, in capitals, had been underlined twice.

Cathy rocked back on her heels, feeling sick. Who would write such a thing?

There was a creak and Cathy looked up, startled.

Swathed in a large white towel, Suzalinna poked her head around the bathroom door. 'What were you saying?'

Cathy's hand closed over the paper, she heard it crumple. Her heart raced but she forced a smile and pointed to the hotel's hair dryer attached to the mirror. 'Why did you bring your own when you must have known they'd have one?'

'Oh, darling, you know how awful those bloody things are. I'm not slumming it for anyone. I knew it would be a pig of a course and I was right, wasn't I? I'm glad I brought a few luxuries now that we're stuck here. You'll be glad in the morning when you borrow it too.'

Her head disappeared once more and Cathy found herself alone, trembling. Had Suzalinna read the note? She assumed not. Her friend would have mentioned it. Suzalinna would have torn it up and thrown it in the bin just as she would do now. Cathy crossed the room and tossed the dreadful message into the basket. The bin was empty save the note. Cathy stood looking down at the fragments of paper. Despite tearing it, the word: 'BITCH' was still visible. 'Oh, God,' Cathy moaned under her breath and bent down again. She couldn't leave it for Suzalinna to see. Cathy slid the bits of crumpled paper into her pocket. In a moment of madness, she toyed with the idea of eating them but no, she'd flush them down the toilet. It was the only way of getting rid of them quickly.

As her friend showered next door, Cathy undressed, her movements jerky and pensive. She couldn't tell Suzalinna. It would only anger and distress her. She sat down heavily on the bed. The springs creaked. It seemed that Kenneth was not the only one who had been digging dirt on the instructors. It surely couldn't have been him who left the nasty note though. After all, why then would he mention on the first night the awful incident of Suzalinna's trainee dying? Cathy assumed that was what the note alluded to. She knew Suzalinna better than most and the death of her medical student was the only incident she could think of that might spark such a poisonous message.

Cathy grimaced at her reflection. A mirror propped up on the chest of drawers opposite her bed showed her pale features, her grey eyes full of unease. But when had the note been left for Suzalinna to find? Had it simply been pushed under the door the previous day leaving her absent-minded friend to step over it, even perhaps kicking it under the bed? Cathy slid her bare feet under the covers and pulled the duvet over her knees. And for what purpose might someone leave such a thing anyway? How did they expect poor Suzalinna to respond?

Cathy heard the drum of water stop and the drip of the shower on the tray. Had anyone else received a note? She thought of Duncan. He might well have been targeted as an instructor also. Cathy cast her mind back to the interactions she had had with the man. Her initial impression had been positive. He had a reassuring confidence about him. But, of course, that had all changed when the police inspector had begun to question him. Then, he had been quite different. Embittered, Cathy thought, and defensive. Had his mood been further darkened by an anonymous letter also? Cathy doubted very much if he'd be willing to admit to it even if she asked outright.

She recalled seeing him in the garden earlier with Jamie. The two of them had been in deep conversation. What had that been about?

Suzalinna was drying herself. Had Kenneth been the recipient of a note too, assuming that he had not been the poison pen?

'I wonder if the police have found anything in Kenneth's room,' she said as Suzalinna opened the bathroom door. A waft of steam entered the bedroom momentarily before the cooler air overpowered it.

'What like, Cath?' Suzalinna asked, rubbing the end of her towel in her ear.

Cathy shrugged. 'I don't know. Maybe, if someone had arranged to meet him in the scenario rooms, there'd be a note.'

'The killer would hardly leave something like that to be found, would they, silly?'

Cathy nodded. 'I suppose not.'

She got up and crossed to the bathroom, closing the door behind her. The bathmat on the floor showed two damp imprints. Cathy lifted it and hung it on the towel rail then, reaching into her pocket, she fished out the bits of paper. Without further consideration, she dropped them into the toilet and flushed. For a moment, she worried that they wouldn't go down, but the final fragment, bobbed and eddied and then, much to her relief, caught in a swirling motion and was dragged down under. Cathy closed the toilet lid with a bang. That was that.

When she came back through, Suzalinna was towelling dry her hair.

'So then, Cathy, have you worked it out yet?'

'What?'

'I thought you'd have plumped for one of them by now. Who do you think killed Kenneth?'

Cathy wrinkled her nose. 'Oh, I don't know. But I meant to ask you about Duncan. He does seem a bit of a dark horse, phoning the department behind your back and so on. I'm wondering about him now.'

Suzalinna turned, her eyebrows arched.

'Try and think hard about the first night before we all arrived,' Cathy urged. 'You were alone with Kenneth and Duncan. You said that Kenneth was being horrible. He made it clear he had looked into your past. I just wonder if he'd done the same with Duncan. Was anything specific said, can you remember?'

'Well, he mentioned Roderick quite soon after I arrived, as it happens. But you mean when it was just the three of us at dinner?'

'Yes.'

'Well, first of all, it sort of wasn't just the three of us.'

Cathy looked at her sharply. 'What do you mean?'

Suzalinna shrugged. 'I'm glad I brought these pyjamas. The waist of my skirt has been cutting in terribly.'

'Suz!' Cathy reached across to grab a pillow.

'All right, all right,' her friend laughed, 'we're a little old for pillow-fights surely. No, I wasn't going to tell you anything exciting. Nothing you didn't already know. It was just that Charles and Joan were there too for the meal.'

'What, at the same table as you?'

Suzalinna began rummaging in her bag and finally found the oversized T-shirt she had been looking for. 'No, silly,' she said. 'They were in the dining room, though, and of course we knew that they were participants and had said a quick hello.'

Cathy sighed. 'I thought you were going to tell me something new. Okay, so, over the meal, you've already said that Kenneth brought up your horrible misfortune with Roderick. What about Duncan though? You've still to tell me in what way Kenneth antagonised him.'

Suzalinna, having found her T-shirt, was now looking for moisturiser. 'It's in here somewhere,' she said to herself and then hearing Cathy's warning, she straightened up. 'Oh, Cathy, there's nothing to say. Kenneth was getting drunker and drunker. He'd said something nasty about one of Duncan's suggestions for the scenario rooms. Duncan didn't back down, as I seem to recall. The two of them were red in the face and glaring at one another across the table. I knew the whole weekend would be an awful drag after that.'

Cathy groaned. 'What I wanted was the suggestion that Kenneth had known something about Duncan from in the past. Maybe something a bit like your Roderick story. That might have given us a motive.'

'Why are you focusing on Duncan? I think the rest of them are more suspicious. Jamie is a very odd one as we've already discussed...'

'I'm not focusing on Duncan,' Cathy said through gritted teeth. 'I really feel as if you're deliberately misunderstanding me. All I wanted was to know who Kenneth had spoken to privately. You said earlier that you couldn't remember anyone from dinner last night and so, it was a natural leap to consider the night before that. The person Kenneth had spent the most time with other than yourself was Duncan.'

'I'm disappointed you haven't worked it out yet,' Suzalinna said, ignoring this and getting into bed.

Cathy groaned. 'Oh, I don't know what to think. Perhaps you're right. I'm losing my touch. Anyway, I'm done going round in circles. Maybe tomorrow, things will look clearer.'

27

'Suz?' Cathy whispered.

There was no reply. Her friend's rhythmical breathing continued. The noise came again. A quiet tap. Cathy lay rigid, listening. Had she imagined it? Now, she was too afraid to move. From outside the room, she thought she heard a creak. A floorboard. Someone was in the corridor. Cathy drew the covers up to her chest and tentatively sat up in bed. Her heart was hammering in her chest and her breathing so shallow she felt dizzy. Perhaps she had dreamt it.

The tap came again and then she was sure she heard the door handle move.

The room was in darkness. Cathy held her breath, trying to focus on the door but unable to see a thing. Slowly, her eyes became more accustomed to the dark. Was someone trying to come in? She peered across at her friend who lay motionless in the bed beside her own. How typical of Suzalinna to sleep through. Although to be fair, Suzalinna had insisted on locking the door and had put a chair under the door handle. 'Just in case someone's got a master key,' she had said before climbing into bed. 'I'm not leaving anything to chance when it comes to you, Cathy.'

Cathy had laughed at the time, but now she was glad Suzalinna had taken the extra precaution. Had the chief inspector put her in danger by openly confiding in her at the start? She looked at the clock on her bedside table. It was 2.15. What on earth was someone doing creeping about at that ungodly hour?

The tap came again and it sounded as if someone was clearing their throat in the corridor outside. She would have to respond in some way. What should she do?

'Suz,' she hissed again.

Suzalinna's breathing changed and the other woman turned over.

'Wake up, idiot,' Cathy said. 'Someone's at our door.'

Her friend sat up in bed. 'What? Who? What do they want?'

Now feeling braver, Cathy threw back the covers and got up. 'I didn't want to answer on my own, given the circumstances,' she said, crossing the room. It was cold and she pulled her dressing gown from the end of the bed. Now, she put her ear to the door and listened again. There was no sound. 'Hello?' Cathy said. No answer. She turned to her friend who had switched on a bedside light.

'I suppose you should open it,' Suzalinna said, rubbing her forehead and yawning. 'Bloody hell, Cathy, have you seen the time?'

Cathy tutted. 'The whole point of locking the door was to stop someone coming in.'

'Now I'm awake, they'd have to murder both of us,' Suzalinna said. 'Open the door and see who it is. Suppose someone's unwell and needs one of us.'

Cathy moved the chair to the side and unlocked the door.

She opened it uncertainly, wondering who she might find on the other side.

The corridor should have been lit all night really, but someone must have turned off the hall lights accidentally. Cathy stared into the darkness.

'Well?' Suzalinna asked, still in bed. 'Who is it and what the hell are they playing at?'

Cathy stepped into the corridor. 'Hello?' she asked, looking up and down but seeing nothing.

The carpeted floor was cold underfoot and there was a draft coming along the long corridor. She shivered and as she stepped further, the door slammed behind her. Cathy spun around, frantically tugging at the handle, afraid of being shut out. The door didn't open. She slapped her palm on the wood and called out. 'Suz, for God's sake open it.'

Now desperate and feeling a fool for being so frightened, she called out again. She heard her friend moaning but spun around, convinced that someone was directly behind.

'What?' she asked. Her voice was shrill.

She stepped backwards, leaning on the door frame, but Suzalinna had opened the door at exactly that moment and she fell into the room.

'Cathy, what are you doing? Anyone would think you were drunk. Get up.'

Cathy rubbed her shoulder, feeling more annoyed than frightened now. What a farce. She'd have a bruise in the morning. She spoke angrily. 'Who is it out there? I've had enough of this. Suz, turn on the corridor light.'

Her friend fumbled along the wall trying to find a switch and finally, the corridor was ablaze with light. The two women blinked. No one was there but a door further along was ajar. It was Cathy's original room, number thirteen.

'Martha?' Cathy hissed, not wanting to wake the entire hotel now over something trivial. Both she and Suzalinna made their way to the open door. 'Martha, were you knocking on our door just now?' Cathy pushed the door but something was wedged against it. She pushed harder and only then, she saw. On the floor, propped up against the door with her back to it, lay Dr Martha Ross. Cathy staggered backwards, her breath coming in heaves.

'Oh God, Oh God, please no!'

But this time, there was no mistaking it.

Suzalinna was at her shoulder. She touched Cathy and gently moved her aside. Then crouching down by the huddled figure, Suzalinna slid her hand under the woman's chin. Martha's head had nodded forward and her hair, lank and greasy, thankfully covered her face.

Suzalinna looked up. 'She's gone, Cathy. There's nothing we can do.'

28

In the end, it was Mary's mother who told him about the tragedy at Sandeels. He had heard snatches of it from Mary but she couldn't bring herself to tell him the full story. Perhaps her mother saw it as her duty before she died. Her husband, Mary's father, had gone to liver cirrhosis the previous year. Drank himself to an early grave, Mary's mother had said bitterly, but it had been true all the same. It was the culture on the island, especially with fishers. Mary's mother had seen her own father do much the same with whisky and this had angered her further.

Back in the day, she had been seen as a great catch for a husband. Her eyes had clouded as she told him, lost in the nostalgia. Daughters of fishers were well known to be far better wives and homemakers than weaver folk. Proper hardworking and smart, everyone knew that. Back then, girls only gained a basic education on the island itself leaving some of the boys to go to the mainland for boarding if their families could afford it. Few did. Taking on the family business of boats or sheep was always the expectation and besides, there were fewer children on the island back then. Now, of course, there was a ferry to the closest island of Tiree, a trip of forty-five minutes on a good day. In winter though, it was unpredictable. Mary, along with her contemporaries, had missed nearly an entire term one year due to the treacherous crossing. Better not to chance it, the ferries said and they were right. Skeln had seen enough tragedies of that kind to last them a lifetime.

'So, what was it all about?' Gus had asked. 'I still can't see why she blames herself. The nightmares are dreadful. I wish she'd just talk to me.'

He had come to the house alone. Mary's mother had suffered a stroke the previous month and she knew without the need of Gus telling her that she had little time left in this world. Usually, in the evening Mary would have come with him but she had been unwell that day also. It was her third miscarriage but they hadn't told her mother she was even expecting after the disappointment of the last two. Better not to raise anyone's hopes this time. Mary didn't need the consoling glances from anyone. At least this way they could recover in private.

He'd left her in the living room, a hot water bottle pressed to her abdomen. They'd get over it. And if it wasn't meant to be... But they both knew a child would have been the cherry on the cake. Their love for one another was never in question and Gus had told her after the second one that they didn't need a baby to cement their marriage at all. She was more than enough for him. Before he had left that evening, she had looked up, her eyes dark with sadness.

'You know this is punishment for Sandeels, don't you?'

He didn't answer but turned and left her there. He felt awful for it but what could he say? As he walked the short distance to his mother-in-law's house, he determined to ask her. It would be awkward for both of them but he had to know.

The elderly woman's face drooped on the right. She lifted a hand to her lips. Her skin was almost translucent blue and the veins a network of converging streams. Her movements were jerky and her speech slurred and painful.

'Sandeels. That day,' she whispered and shook her head.

'She's already told me a little,' Gus said, hoping to spare her some effort. 'There were three of them? All just children. Mary was there with this Rebecca friend she had from the island. But there was another girl. Mary told me she was only visiting for a holiday?'

Mary's mother nodded. 'Yes. Rare.'

'Yes. I understand. Tourists were quite unusual back then. Well, they still are now. But this girl's family were staying for a few weeks? Mary had befriended her but something went wrong. There was a bit of an argument, was there?'

Mary's mother nodded, her eyes watering. 'Trouble with girls,' she said slowly. 'Boys're easier.'

Gus smiled.

'Out too far,' she said suddenly. Her hand stretched in a jerk before her. It fluttered and fell to her lap.

'They went swimming?' Gus asked patiently. 'Mary, her island friend and this holidaymaker girl? Did they go out too far though? I know Mary's a strong swimmer even now but it was this other girl, the one not from the island, who got into difficulty?'

Mary's mother nodded. 'Yes. Drowning.'

'And yet it wasn't her who lost her life?'

The old woman shook her head.

'It was Rebecca?'

'Becca. Known from a baby.'

'It still plays on Mary's mind. Seeing anyone drown must be terrible, especially given their age but her best friend... It sounds like she nearly drowned herself too.'

'Fishers.'

'There'd been a boat not far off, yes, she said. But why then does she blame herself for it? I don't understand. It was a tragic accident surely and she and this other girl were lucky to walk away themselves. The sea can be cruel even to the most experienced swimmer.'

'Talk.'

Gus shook his head not understanding. 'Talk?'

'Afterwards. Talk.'

'About what? Admittedly they were silly to go out swimming that day perhaps but...'

'The boatman. He saw.'

'Saw what? I don't understand.'

'Becca went under. She was beside her. Pushed her under.'

'But why would she?'

'Held Becca down. Jealous of Becca. Wanted her to herself. They said murder.'

Gus sat back in stunned silence.

The old woman shook her head. 'Sad. Sad for Mary. Police asked but nothing more.'

He nodded. 'Surely the boatman was mistaken though. It can't have been.'

Mary's mother died a week later. Gus never spoke of Sandeels again and the only time he heard Mary mention it was in her dreams, kicking at the bedcovers in suffocating fear. Haunted even as an adult by her childhood ghosts.

29

'Dr Moreland,' the chief inspector said. 'Be as precise as you can. Exactly what made you wake?'

Cathy wrapped the loose-fitted jumper more tightly around herself. She glanced up at the clock. It was four thirty. They sat in the room in which the detective had interviewed her and the other guests only hours before over Kenneth Docherty's death. Now, here she was again but this time, it was because of Martha Ross.

In the end, Mr Faber had called the police and, giving up any hope of sleep for the rest of the night, Cathy and Suzalinna had waited in the lobby to be questioned. The rest of the guests slept on in blissful ignorance despite the atrocity only metres from all their rooms. Of course, one person might be only too well aware of what had happened. After all, someone had killed Martha. Someone had crept along the corridor and stabbed her, then presumably, they had retreated to their room to feign sleep. Cathy shuddered at the thought of it. How would the murderer behave in the morning? Would they put on a show of distress when they heard the news?

The chief inspector cleared his throat. He had already

explained their preliminary findings. It seemed that poor Martha had been stabbed quite brutally in her back but worse than that, the murderer had chosen to use a piece of medical kit as their weapon. The equipment was still to be identified by the police surgeon but from the way he had described it, Cathy thought it sounded very much like a chest drain needle. How utterly horrible and so telling to choose such an instrument when anything might have done. Suzalinna had been explaining chest drain insertion only two days before. Cathy recalled holding the wide-bore needle during the demonstration. It must have been four inches long and brutal as a weapon if the perpetrator elected to use it that way. Suzalinna had only brought the chest drains as a matter of interest too. It had been explained that in an emergency, they would be unlikely to fit a full drain but instead, they should simply use a venflon if someone had a tension pneumothorax.

'Dr Moreland?'

Cathy swallowed. Her stomach had a hollow nauseous feeling. So much had happened since the life-support course. 'I thought I heard someone outside our door,' she said.

He motioned for her to expand, but she sat silently once more thinking over the events of the night and recalling the horrible note she had found in Suzalinna's room. What could she tell the chief inspector anyway? She had thought she was dreaming at first when she heard the tap on their door in the middle of the night. Suzalinna had slept through, not hearing a thing. There would be very little her friend could tell the police when she was questioned after Cathy. They had found Martha together but that was it. They'd seen no one else at all, other than when they came downstairs to alert the hotel staff.

It couldn't have been Martha tapping on their door and turning the handle. She had surely been dead for some time. Who, then, had tried to rouse her and Suzalinna and for what reason? Had someone discovered Martha before them? Had they tried to get help? Or was it something else entirely? Perhaps night-time was when someone had come to confide some piece of evidence or suspicion so as not to be observed by the rest of the group. Had Jamie or Ryan seen something strange on the night of Kenneth's death? Was it one of them who had knocked and tried to come into their room? But why choose the middle of the night? There had to be other opportunities. The garden was a quiet enough place for private discussions. Why not talk there the following day?

Cathy shook her head at her unvoiced questions. Perhaps it had all been her imagination, but it didn't change the fact that a woman lay dead. Cathy must have woken because of some sound.

She had already explained to the chief inspector about her decision to change rooms and share with her old medical school friend instead of Martha. At first, he had seemed surprised but she wasn't going to go into the ins and outs of it with him. She and Martha hadn't got on particularly well but she was aware that saying it to the police officer was like an admission of guilt. She looked up. He had clicked his pen twice as if to hurry her along.

'I'm sorry,' she said. 'I'm a bit all over the place. You wanted to know about me waking up? I'll be frank, I'm a light sleeper. Even on the first night here, before any wrongdoing occurred, I found it difficult to drop off. The hotel gave me the creeps. I guess, what with Kenneth's death, I was on edge last night. I felt we were all looking at each other suspiciously and with good reason. We barricaded the door in case something like this happened.'

'Barricaded the door? Was there a particular reason why you thought someone else might be at risk? I assume you thought you or Dr Bhat would be the next intended victim?'

Cathy folded her arms. She wanted to say that in asking for her help with the investigation at the start, he had put her in potential danger, but it wasn't just that. She considered and then decided she must say. 'There was a note.'

The chief inspector looked at her sharply. 'A note?'

'Well, I've not even told her. I suppose I really should have by now. I was trying to save any further upset. It made me uneasy though, of course. Who would do such a thing?'

'Dr Moreland?'

Cathy swallowed and tried hard to focus her attention fully on the question she was being asked. Repeatedly, her mind wandered back to the dreadful moment when they discovered Martha. Suzalinna's hand touching the girl's grey skin and then her friend's horrified expression when she realised that she was beyond help.

'Dr Moreland? There was a note? Can you explain what you mean?'

'Earlier that evening,' Cathy said, rubbing her forehead as if trying to obliterate the image in her mind. 'It was after dinner and Suzalinna and I went up early. I'd not yet moved my stuff to the room so I nipped along to collect my bag.'

'You had previously been sharing with Dr Ross, you said?'

'That's right but as you know, Suzalinna and I were friends long before and we thought it would be nice to bunk in together. At the start, Martha had made it quite clear that she'd rather have a room to herself.'

'Go on.'

'When I went back to Suzalinna's room, she decided to have a shower. It's a twin room and as she'd been on her own the previous two nights, she had spread out a good deal. While she was in the bathroom, I moved some of her things and as I did so, I saw it on the floor. I assume that without realising it was there, she'd kicked the piece of folded paper under the bed I was meant to be sleeping in. I've no idea when it was slid under the door. I assume that would be how it was delivered.'

'What did the note say?'

Cathy grimaced, not wanting to repeat the horrible words. 'I chucked it, of course. Tore it up and flushed it down the toilet.'

'Dr Moreland?'

Cathy sighed. 'It alluded to Roderick if you must know. It didn't mention his name but the message was clear. *How do you sleep at night?* Or something equally nasty. Poor Suz was distressed already having to speak about it to you yesterday. We, of course, know that Kenneth had found out about the awful incident but it seems that someone else in the hotel knew also.'

'There was no request for money? No attempt to use the information as a bargaining tool?'

Cathy shook her head. 'It was simply a vindictive message. I've no idea what purpose it was meant to serve. I thought about it when I was trying to get to sleep last night. I suppose the only motive for leaving it was to upset Suzalinna. Now that Martha's dead, I wonder if the killer and note leaver are the same person. Might they have been trying to drive Suzalinna to suicide? If they knew her, they wouldn't have bothered. Suz is rock solid. Nothing like that would faze her.'

'And yet, you didn't show her the note?'

Cathy nodded. 'Yes, you're right, but not because she's so fragile she couldn't take it. It was because I was angry. I was furious. Why should she have to read that? Now I wonder, of course, if other people have received nasty letters...'

'We'll look into it. Now, getting back to last night, can you explain what it was that made you think someone was outside your room in the corridor?'

Cathy wondered if he'd think she was being over-imaginative but she had to speak the truth. 'I thought someone knocked on the door.' She smiled slightly. 'It sounds silly now, but I thought the handle turned too.'

He raised his eyebrows.

'I know it sounds fanciful and perhaps I was spooked. I woke Suzalinna. We turned on the lights in the room and I got up to see.'

The chief inspector nodded. 'And?'

'Well, nothing. No one was there, but when we turned on the lights, the door along the corridor was open. It was the room I had originally shared with Martha, of course, and I thought it was odd.'

'So, you went to see what was going on?'

'And found her, yes.'

The chief inspector sighed. 'I'll admit it's a tricky situation, Dr Moreland. I'm sure you of all people must understand my difficulty having been involved in such things in the past before.'

'Tricky? Well, that's putting it mildly. There's a killer upstairs right now, pretending to be fast asleep in their bed. Come morning, they'll waltz downstairs and pretend to be horrified at the news.'

The chief inspector cleared his throat and shifted in his seat.

'What?' Cathy asked, recognising his discomfort. 'What is it?'

'Well, it's just this. These deaths have occurred in very particular circumstances. I have two suspicious deaths, both of which have a very strong medical element to them by the looks of things. Not only that but both you and Dr Bhat have been present at the discovery of each. If you look at it from my point of view, Dr Moreland, it does look rather odd, wouldn't you agree? Now, Kenneth Docherty went out of his way to antagonise your friend, Dr Bhat. He humiliated her by bringing up a rather unsavoury incident from the past. Dr Docherty was then found dead the following day. Then, we have Martha Ross. I spoke with Martha as you know. I won't go into what she said but I don't think it'll be a surprise to know that she didn't speak too favourably.'

'Of me? Well, I knew she had an issue with something but I still don't know what the problem was. How can I answer to it if I don't know what she said?'

The chief inspector shook his head. 'You'll see how awkward this is. Two people who have slighted you either directly or indirectly have been found dead. Yes, I'd say it makes things rather awkward.'

30

'He can't suspect us, Cath, and if he does, he'll soon come to his senses.'

They were sitting together in the dining room.

'The only person who's been nice about it all is Mr Faber,' Suzalinna continued. 'I know we thought he was a bit creepy at first but did you see how he was?'

Cathy nodded. The hotel owner had indeed done all that he could to be comforting and helpful. He had suggested that they might prefer to move room. He had another currently on a different corridor and he'd open it for them if they'd rather. Cathy had said that this was not necessary. She hoped that they'd not have to spend another night there at all. But in any case, he had instead insisted on bringing them breakfast in the dining room and pouring cups of over-brewed tea for them both.

'I'm going to call Chris,' Cathy said suddenly, sliding her chair back.

Suzalinna looked at the clock on the wall. It was six forty-five. 'He'll be coming off night shift soon. Why not leave it?'

'I want to catch him before he goes to bed.'

Suzalinna sighed. 'I guess we won't be getting any sleep now.'

'Could you honestly even try?' Cathy asked.

'The rest of them will be waking up soon anyway. I wonder what they'll all say.'

'Some of them might have heard. The police were trying to be quiet but there have been half a dozen people traipsing up and down those stairs. Jamie's room is only three doors down from ours. Unless he took a sleeping tablet, he can't have failed to know something odd's going on.'

'I doubt he'd open his door to find out even if he did think someone was in trouble. What a mouse of a man,' Suzalinna said. 'Out of all of them, he has been the most pathetic, hasn't he? There's no way he's the killer anyway. No guts whatsoever.'

Cathy nodded. 'He's not done himself any favours really, I suppose. Joan said something funny about him yesterday as it happens. She said that Charles had compared him to a GP trainee he had mentored years ago.'

Suzalinna raised her eyebrows.

'Apparently, the doctor in question was struck off,' Cathy finished. 'I don't know what Charles saw in Jamie to make him think that. Maybe like you say it's his mousiness, his way of being both pitiful and annoying at the same time. Not a good combination for a nurse practitioner and obviously not for a doctor either. I'd like to find out more about Jamie. I saw him talking to Duncan in the garden yesterday and I want to know what it was about. They looked very serious.'

'You've moved from Duncan to him, have you?'

'I think they're all potentials and yet at the same time, I can't believe any of them would do it. Each of us is medically trained to save lives, not end them. Anyway,' she sighed, 'I'm going to get Chris busy on our behalf.'

'Oh? I thought you were simply phoning for moral support after what happened last night?'

Cathy shook her head. 'That, of course, but no. I need to get him to do a bit of digging. The internet seems to be down here. I asked Andrea at reception when we arrived and she said something about the wifi being intermittent due to the remoteness of the hotel.'

'What do you want him to look into?'

'I'm interested in a bit of geographical information,' Cathy said obscurely. 'But while I'm settling that, perhaps you can do something for me.'

Suzalinna flopped back in her seat. 'Me? Well, I'll try my best. Name it, darling.'

'Could you give Brodie a ring? I assume he's contactable just now?'

Brodie was Suzalinna's colleague, a senior registrar in Glainkirk General and soon to be a consultant if a position made itself available. Suzalinna spoke highly of him and he'd get an excellent reference from her. Cathy had met him on several occasions for work nights out. She had spoken to him on the phone referring patients to the department also.

'What do you want from poor overworked Brodie?' Suzalinna asked. 'He's probably in a huff with me for abandoning him to go on this bloody course.'

'It'll be awkward but I'd like to know about Duncan. I realise he's not a paramedic in our area but I'm sure Brodie could make a few calls...'

Suzalinna looked doubtful. 'What should I say we're looking for?'

Cathy considered. It was hard to know. 'Anything unusual, I suppose.' And to Suzalinna's pained expression, she sighed. 'I'm after any reason someone might find to blackmail him. A bit of a dodgy past, something untoward that he'd rather wasn't dragged up, although, as yet, I've no idea why anyone would want to do such a thing. We've said already that this course seems to have been more important to some participants than others. I have a feeling someone has been doing a bit of investigative work for themselves already. I think it began well before the course started. All of the instructors seem to have been fair game. If someone badly needed to pass, I wonder if they made double sure by finding out anything negative about their assessors. Perhaps to blackmail them if necessary.'

'Well, this blackmailing idiot would've been pretty disappointed when they looked into my murky past. There's nothing to find out about me,' Suzalinna said, her bottom lip petulant.

Cathy turned to her friend. 'But don't you see, that's where you're wrong? There was Roderick. I'm sorry to bring it up again, Suz, but to a spitefully-minded individual, that rather unsavoury incident might well have been useful blackmail fodder. Oh, don't look like that,' Cathy said in response to Suzalinna's obvious disgust. 'Someone's murdered twice here. What would a little blackmail amount to in comparison? It'd be nothing. Listen, I've no idea what their motive is as yet, but the more we know about everyone here, the better. Two people are dead. I've no idea why they were killed or by whom but I'm very much afraid that the murderer has already thrown caution to the wind. Once you've killed twice, the taboo is lost rather, isn't it?'

31

Chris was horrified when she finally managed to get through and all but insisted on coming to the hotel to collect Cathy whether the chief inspector allowed it or not.

'Don't be ridiculous,' she scolded, secretly rather pleased to have provoked the reaction.

When he was then asked if he'd mind doing a little investigative work on her behalf, he groaned. 'Seriously, Cathy? I thought you were going to let the police look into things themselves from now on.'

'He's pretty much accused me and Suzalinna!' She exploded and then fearing that someone might overhear despite being in her bedroom with the door firmly closed, she lowered her voice. 'I'm not asking much. Listen, Suzalinna's getting Brodie to look into things too. We can't just sit back and wait for the police to go through the motions again. I was willing to do that at the start but look where that got us. The chief inspector seems a decent sort of man but all he seemed to do yesterday was haul each of us in and get very little for his trouble. He's got it in for me and Suz. I'd say we're his main suspects. I've still to find out what Martha said about me. God knows it must have been pretty damning. I just have a bad feeling about this. He said there was going to be a police presence in the hotel last night. How then did Martha end up getting stabbed? I don't like it, Chris. It feels clinical, like it's been carefully planned.'

He sighed. 'All right then. Tell me what you want and I'll try.'

Cathy explained.

'I can't promise anything,' he replied. 'I'm no use at this sort of thing, you know?'

'It's just a few internet searches and maybe a couple of phone calls,' Cathy pleaded. 'I'd do it myself but there's no internet here. It's so frustrating. You'd think it was an essential part of having a hotel. Without wifi, we're completely isolated.'

Chris snorted. 'Even if the phones went down, I have no doubt you'd find a way, Cathy. I don't recall you being like this at all at medical school. You were so quiet. So timid.'

Cathy was again reminded of Jamie the young nurse practitioner who she had called mouse-like on more than one occasion now. 'Before you go, Chris, there's just one other thing...'

———

Downstairs, the rest of the group had gathered. When she entered the room, Cathy immediately found her eyes going to Ryan who was closest to the door. They all appeared to be in shock, which was little wonder, but his face had an almost haunted quality. Cathy wondered if there had been a connection between him and Martha after all. She had suspected it a couple of times over the two days. The way Ryan had pulled out Martha's chair, the way he had gone to help her carry her plate of sandwiches. If he hadn't known her before the course, he had been making a real effort to become acquainted. Well, if he had planned to woo her, any romance had been cut short.

Cathy found her eyes wandering over the other faces, her contemporaries. Joan was standing close to Charles. He rested a hand protectively on the small of his wife's back, his face was pale and serious. To their left was Duncan, arms folded. Cathy wondered if it was in self-defence. It was certainly a telling gesture for a man who had once been at least partly in charge of running the course. Now he was on the same level as the rest. A suspect. As much in the frame for murder as all of them. Then there was Jamie. In some ways, Cathy was surprised to see him there. Perhaps now, the chief inspector wouldn't let any of them out of his sight. There would be no more allowances. No more lenience.

By the window, an unobtrusive uniformed officer stood. He had looked across as Cathy had entered but now pretended to focus his attention on a picture above the fireplace. Jamie nodded at her. Of all of the group, she seemed to be the only one to have dodged his disdain. Unlike the rest, he was seated. He had positioned his chair at an odd angle, facing slightly off centre, and more in line with the window than the rest of the room. It was as if he was both physically and metaphorically giving them the cold shoulder.

The door opened and Suzalinna and the chief inspector came in. Cathy had seen them speaking in the hall. She had no idea what was being said. Suzalinna had answered all of his questions earlier as far as she knew.

The chief inspector cleared his throat. 'Ladies and gentlemen,' he began.

Ryan snorted. He was rubbing the back of his neck. 'Cut the niceties, chief inspector. One of us isn't as principled as all that, after all.'

'I realise it's been a shock, Dr Oliver,' the chief inspector said, nodding slightly. 'If we can remain civil, that will be of benefit. I intend to make this process as painless for all as possible, but I must ask each of you for your whereabouts yesterday evening and night–'

'Ridiculous,' Charles interrupted, almost spitting the word under his breath.

Everyone turned to look at the elderly GP dressed in tweeds, who had now taken a step away from his wife. Charles thrust his chest out in defiance seeing that the attention was now on him alone. 'Well, it is, isn't it? You know where we all were. One of your officers was meant to be watching us. We were here. No one left the hotel. We had dinner together and then we all went to our rooms.'

'One of us didn't,' Ryan said. His eyes were cold and his mouth held a cruel sneer. 'One of us was prowling around in the dead of night again but this time they were sticking wide-bore needles into innocent people.'

Joan, who had not yet spoken, let out a moan. Charles reached out a hand to her but she batted him away. 'For God's sake, stop,' she cried. 'All of you. Just shut up and let the chief inspector speak, will you?' She looked at her husband. 'This was meant to be a fresh start. Our dream...' her words petered out.

Cathy felt as if they were all eavesdropping on a private conversation. The room fell silent.

By the door, the chief inspector moved. 'Dr Oliver? Perhaps if you'd like to come through first.'

'What if I say no?' Ryan challenged. 'Am I under house arrest? Are any of us? What if I say no to any more of this nonsense? What if I tell you I want to leave, I want to pack my bags now and head home? I assume there would be nothing you could do to stop me?'

The chief inspector began to answer but he was interrupted.

'I'd like to go home too,' Jamie stated and getting up, he seemed to stagger slightly. 'I'm happy to co-operate with questions but I refuse to stay in this place any longer waiting to see who'll be next. It won't be me,' he said, moving to the door. As he passed Ryan, he paused. 'And while we're all here, I'd like to say in front of everyone that I know what you've been trying to do.'

Ryan shook his head in disgust.

'You think I'm a fool but I'm not,' Jamie said. 'I've seen what's been happening and I know.'

The rest of the group stared in dumbfounded silence.

Jamie's face was white. Even his lips were colourless.

'What a scene.' Ryan laughed. 'I've no idea what you're talking about.'

Jamie stood, breathing heavily, his hand on the door frame.

'Well,' Charles said heavily. 'If everyone else is leaving, I'd like to take my wife away from here also. We're happy to supply contact details and to talk with you before we go, chief inspector. I see no reason to keep us here. We've tried to be as reasonable and patient as possible, but although I agree little with that young man on anything, I do think that so far this investigation has been haphazard and somewhat lacking. Whoever heard of keeping witnesses or potential suspects, if that's what you want to call us, shut up together like this? It's like some dreadful Agatha Christie trash, not something in modern-day policing. And look where it's left us. Up until yesterday afternoon, I was still under the impression that Kenneth's death had been some kind of dreadful accident. This new and frankly grisly discovery today has pushed any such romantic notions aside. I'm not being obstructive, I hope you realise that, but I feel this has gone beyond the point of reason.' He had taken Joan's elbow, but Joan pulled away and was looking wildly at the detective.

The chief inspector seemed unruffled and nodded as if he had come to much the same conclusion. 'I agree. Things have indeed passed the point of reason and fairness, Dr McKinley. But you have to remember that this is a very serious crime. I'll speak to everyone briefly to confirm contact details and then I'll let you get on your way. Of course, it will slow things down a good deal and we will have to be in touch with each of you again over the next twenty-four hours. During that time, you may well be asked to go to your local police station for formal questioning.'

Joan was still open-mouthed. 'We can't go home. The course. We have to finish. The certificate.' She looked from Duncan to the chief inspector. 'You know one of us is responsible and you're letting us go? You're not charging anyone? I won't have this hanging over me. I can't.'

'I have no concrete evidence to charge anyone, Dr McKinley. Your husband is quite right. I am in no position to insist that you stay here against your will. I had hoped that this matter would have been cleared up quickly. If it is of interest, we did have the post-mortem results back on Dr Docherty. You raised the question as to whether it was accidental?' He said, turning to Charles. 'No, in a word, is the answer. Dr Docherty, along with now, Dr Ross, was deliberately killed. It might have been a good deal easier to have you all in the hotel to speak to about this now double-murder, but I can see that this might not be possible or reasonable to ask of you. After I speak to each of you, unless any new information comes to light, you may leave on the condition that you stay at the address you supply us. We will be in touch to speak with each of you further.'

Joan shook her head. 'I'm not leaving.'

'But, Joan, a double-murder...' her husband began.

She turned on him. 'I realise that, Charles, I'm not stupid. You don't have to keep saying the word murder again and again. Well?' She challenged. 'Which one of you did it? It was one of us; that's what the police think.' Her eyes darted around the room, falling on each of them. When she looked at Cathy, she shook her head sadly. 'Awful.' Her words were almost inaudible.

'Awful. Two lives cut short. Who would do it? And why?' She returned to the chief inspector who stood by the door. 'I'm not leaving. I want the truth to come out. I'm not running away from here with my name in question. I couldn't stand it.'

'She has a point,' Duncan said quietly.

The rest of the group was silent, each of them thinking over what she had said.

'I'll stay,' Suzalinna offered.

Cathy turned to her friend in surprise. 'Saj'll have kittens if he knows you were allowed to leave and didn't.'

Suzalinna shrugged. 'You're staying with me though, aren't you? We'll be fine. I agree with Joan, it seems ridiculous to all go our separate ways with suspicion hanging over us. Duncan? I don't mind talking to you about the course also. If in between the police interviews, members of the group would rather have some resus tuition with a view to doing an informal assessment later for certification, I'll happily agree. What else is there to do?'

32

C hris was apologetic. He had not yet managed to find anything out about one of her leads but he did have some interesting information about one of the course participants. A newspaper article from eighteen months ago had been quite revealing. He said he had found it by doing a simple internet search, looking for any articles on medical errors in the area she had told him. Within thirty minutes he found it, having scrolled through a whole lot of vindictive patient participation group complaints about GP surgeries not having enough face-to-face appointments.

'It doesn't name him,' Chris said. 'Of course, the paper probably couldn't do that, but it is suspicious, isn't it? It's where he works, after all, and it would fit. Well, what do you think? Have I done well?'

Cathy told him that he had all but solved the whole thing.

He laughed. 'Don't be like that. I'll get onto the other matter later. I need to sleep now. Last night was hellish. A nasty RTA. Ortho did their stuff, and that left us picking up the pieces. I was in theatre half the night.' His voice was strained.

Cathy felt a pang of guilt. He was going through a difficult time himself and she was unable to offer him the support he deserved. Before she hung up, she tried to tell him how she felt. 'Chris, you are okay, aren't you?'

He snorted. 'Don't worry about me, Cath. You sort yourself out. But please look after yourself and Suzalinna. I hate the pair of you staying on there. At least I'm in no immediate danger at work. You, on the other hand... Listen, Cath, I don't want to be funny with you over this but please can you leave this to the police now? I don't like it at all. I have a horrible feeling about it.'

'I don't want to beat about the bush, Jamie. I think there have already been enough misunderstandings to last us a lifetime,' Cathy said.

They walked side-by-side. She had told him that the best place was the garden. No corners to hide behind and no doors to listen at. Maybe she was being unfair and appealing to his paranoid state but in part, she spoke the truth.

Jamie had nodded in agreement. 'Yes, I can see that. Best get away from the place. You never know who might be listening.'

'Just as you did with Duncan the other day? When the two of you had a chat?'

He looked sideways at her. 'Yes. Something like that.'

They paused at the end of the path that led from the conservatory past a border of well-tended flowers. Cathy turned and looked back at the house. It was on the same side as her and Suzalinna's bedroom. On the other side of the corridor, she knew that the police would still be at work assessing the scene of the crime. Poor Martha.

'You know that I have unfortunately been involved with things like this in the past? One of the doctors at my practice was killed a couple of years ago. I helped the police then. I'd like to help them now if the chief inspector would listen.'

Jamie nodded. 'They were talking about you at breakfast, the rest of them.'

She looked keenly at him. 'Jamie, I'm sorry to put you on the spot but why did Martha take such a dislike to me? Joan mentioned that she hadn't been too complimentary on the first day of the course. Had you heard her reasoning?'

'Oh, the drugs, I assume.'

'Excuse me?'

'Sorry to be so blunt, but you want the truth, don't you? You said no beating about the bush and I want to get home as fast as anyone. Martha knew you were a drug user. Listen, it's none of my business and maybe it's in the past. We all have a history after all but...'

Cathy shook her head in disbelief. 'But, Jamie, it's not true. I don't use illicit drugs.'

'Stolen prescription ones? That's what she said. Look, I don't want to make things awkward. She's dead now, after all.'

Cathy's face flushed. 'My God.'

'I told you, it's none of my business and I don't want to know if it's true or not. I didn't know you before this course and we'll never see one another again after it either. If you can sort this mess out faster than that police detective, I don't care if you are shooting up in the toilets daily. Like I say, I want to go home and I want this whole thing done with.'

Cathy had felt suddenly cold. The cruelty was that there was truth in what he said. It was long ago and in the very first stages of her mental illness. She had indeed taken co-codamol from the practice store cupboard to calm her mania. Her practice partners had found out. Changes had been made. When she was well enough to return to work, safeguards had been put in place so that it couldn't happen again. That had been five years ago.

She had moved on from it, they all had. It had been dealt with and she was stable and had never been tempted to do such a thing again. How then, had Martha found out?

Jamie was looking at her. 'Well, what did you want to ask me? I assume it wasn't about that.'

Cathy tried to gather her thoughts. She swallowed and shook her head. 'No, it wasn't but for the record, I don't take any drugs, Jamie. Martha walked in on me when I was taking some paracetamol for my migraine. I can only assume that she misunderstood.'

He shrugged. 'Whatever.'

'I wanted to ask what made you decide to come here for the course? You said already that there was a situation. You felt out of control and you didn't want to feel that way again? I just wondered if it had something to do with the tension between you and Ryan. When you spoke to him just now, you seemed very angry.'

'I was angry and I am still. I think if any one of us is a killer, it's that man.'

'Jamie...' She was unsure how he would react but she had to know. 'A child. I'm sorry to ask this. A child died...?'

He seemed to shrink back from her. 'You too? God!'

'Jamie, please believe me, I'm not accusing you of anything. I'm not trying to hurt you at all.'

He turned away.

'Jamie, please. I think someone else knew. I think there's been a lot of planning and someone had researched all of us before we arrived here. The child's death was tragic but if there had been any negligence on your part, you would no longer be allowed to practice. I assume there was an investigation? You must have been through a terrible time.'

Her words seemed to finally hit home. His posture changed from stiff and distrustful. Now, he allowed his arms to drop to his sides. His shoulders hung loose. 'The worst year of my life,' he whispered.

'Come, let's sit down,' she suggested. By the path, was a stone bench. They walked together to it. 'It was to do with some confusion over an immunisation injection?'

He nodded. His eyes were full of pain. 'Yes. An awful misunderstanding. The mother had told reception about the allergy, but it hadn't been passed on and when I asked her myself, she was distracted. The baby was crying...' Jamie let out a shuddering breath.

'You gave the vaccine in good faith but the child had an anaphylactic reaction?' Cathy could just imagine the horror he must have felt. She had seen a similar thing happen but it had been on a paediatric ward with all of the hospital specialists around and ready to jump in and help. Alone in the community, with little backup or knowledge must have been appalling.

Jamie ran a hand across his forehead. 'Yes. Anaphylactic shock. I wasn't prepared. The mother was screaming and she had her baby in the room too. All the noise.' He closed his eyes tight, his breathing, irregular. 'Oh God, Cathy! It was awful. I called for help. Our resus trolley wasn't equipped for a child arrest though. The ambulance seemed to take forever.'

'I'm sorry.'

'Don't feel sorry for me. His family. They lost a child and it was because of me.'

'Jamie, it wasn't because of you at all. It was a dreadful accident.'

'I'll never get over it. Never. I thought this course would help. I'd decided to move away too. Some nights when I lie awake, I wonder if I should end it myself. I can't sleep. If I close my eyes, I see his face, white. His lips, purple...'

'So that's what you were doing the night of Kenneth's death? You went outside because you couldn't sleep?'

He nodded. 'Not that I can prove it, but I didn't see anything or anyone, Cathy. That's the truth. I wish I had seen bloody Ryan, that vicious creature of a man. I wish I could tell the police I'd seen him sneaking down the corridor with Kenneth. But I...'

'Jamie,' Cathy interrupted firmly. 'Did you receive a note?'

He looked at her in surprise. 'But how did you know?'

'I assume it was in your room? What did it say, if you don't mind telling me?'

'I knew right away. "*Child killer.*" That's all it said. It had to be Ryan. He left it. He's had it in for me from the start. His sort prey on people like me. They sniff us out. Smell our insecurities and when they find them, they won't let up. It's like a game. Like poking a stick at an injured animal.'

Cathy nodded. 'Jamie, did you keep the note?'

'I tore it up and threw it away. But I still can't see how you knew. I didn't tell anyone except Duncan.'

'So that was why you were talking with him in the garden? You told him you had received an anonymous letter. But why did you choose to confide in him?'

'He's about the only one who bothered with me. Even that snooty friend of yours was laughing behind my back during the course. Oh, she tried to help but I could see that she thought I was stupid. Duncan took an interest in me. He explained things differently. Slowed down and didn't make me panic like the rest. When I'm in front of all of you, I clam up. I could feel myself getting worse and worse on that first day. Ryan seemed to know. He enjoyed watching me squirm.'

Cathy nodded. 'I'm sorry it's been such a bad experience for you. But the note. Can I ask that for now at least, you keep this between you and me? Obviously, Duncan knows too but let's leave it at that. I have a feeling our poison pen is responsible for a lot more than just vindictive letter writing and I don't want to provoke them. Thank you for being so honest with me. I appreciate it.' She got up. 'Oh, and for what it's worth, we're not all egomaniacs. Some doctors are shy. Some of us are quite nice people. I don't like these events either. I panic and say the wrong thing. That's why I gabble on so much when I'm first introduced. Anyway, let's hope this is cleared up and we can all get away from here. I doubt any of us will come back to Huntington Lodge in a hurry.'

33

'Why didn't you tell me?' Suzalinna's eyes narrowed. 'We've been friends long enough, for God's sake. I thought you'd have a bit more respect.'

Cathy sighed. 'It was for that very reason I didn't say. I wanted to spare you the worry.'

'It was addressed to me! It had my name on it.'

'Suz, it was a folded scrap of paper. I wasn't ripping open envelopes or reading private correspondence. I wish you'd understand.'

'Well, I suppose I have little choice but to accept it. And you chucked it, did you? That was vital evidence, Cathy. What were you thinking? I'd have thought with your experience you'd have more sense. The chief inspector will be furious when he knows. He already thinks we're up to something as it is. I assume you are going to tell him?'

Cathy looked out of the window. In the distance, she saw Joan and Charles walking along the path that she and Jamie had just returned by.

'Cathy?'

She sighed. 'Well, that's what I wanted to discuss with you.'

'Cathy! We have to tell him. I know it looks odd but I can't see we have any choice. You're worried that he'll think you've tampered with evidence?'

'I did tell him. I'm sorry. I told him before you. I agree that I messed things up throwing the note away and it probably added to his case against us. I'm sorry, okay?'

Suzalinna grimaced. 'It's a bit late for that. He knows about Roderick already anyway. A spiteful note about it can't harm my reputation any further, can it?'

'I wonder...' Cathy said.

'Wonder what?'

Cathy grimaced. 'It just occurred to me. I've been wondering all this while who else might have received a note. You did, Jamie certainly did. I wonder if Martha did too, but rather than an accusation, I wonder if hers was a disclosure about me, her roommate. Was that why her attitude to me changed so quickly?'

'Well, if that is the case, she must have done the same thing as you.'

Cathy raised her eyebrows in question.

'Maybe she read *your* note. Perhaps two notes were in the room, pushed under the door. What if she opened hers and then realised that yours must be of the same ilk and read it also? You assumed that you didn't get one yourself, but maybe you did. You just never saw it.'

Cathy nodded. 'You might well be right. I wish we could get a look in the room and see if we could find it.'

'If the police are still dusting for fingerprints, or whatever it is they're up to, you'll hardly be able to get in there.'

'Maybe we need to ask the others. It's a little awkward. I mean, if they have received a note, it's for a reason and admitting to getting one essentially means disclosing something dreadful about their past that they'd far rather stayed there.' Cathy sighed. 'I don't suppose you got anything from Brodie yet? He was going to be my route to finding out about Duncan. I still feel that there's something strange there.'

'Oh, so you've still got it in for him. Have you? I like Duncan. He's been a real pillar of strength what with everyone trying to beg certificates so that they can complete the course. Charles and Joan have been simply awful haranguing us while they wait. I think if anyone needs to explain themselves it's them. No, Duncan's a good guy, Cathy. He's dealt with all of the departmental communications too. Saved me a lot of work really.'

'I'd love to know if he got a note but you're right. Charles and Joan seem far more desperate than he does. Are you going to finish the course with them, then? I think Jamie would benefit from it too. He's had a terrible time of things and I think he sees this course as closure. He genuinely wants to do the right thing and upskill so he's never in that awful situation of not knowing what to do again. I do realise he's made himself a bit of a loner here. He's not the easiest to like but if anyone deserves a bit of a break, it's him.'

Suzalinna nodded. 'I think we will. Duncan was in talking to the chief inspector about it just now and we'll see what he has to say. As far as I'm concerned, it's fine. I'll go over any questions folk need to ask and Duncan might run through the resus protocol once more. We'll see if we can use one of the scenario rooms again and make it a very straightforward practical assessment. I assume you're not bothered about it now?'

Cathy shook her head. 'I couldn't bring myself to do it, Suz. I'll complete it another time. Not now though. It wouldn't seem right and there never was any urgency in me doing the course. You concentrate on helping the people who need it.'

'Charles will be over the moon.'

'Yes, I need to speak to him. He mentioned that he would be

willing to talk if it meant clearing things up faster. I think now might well be the time to take him up on his offer. I have a feeling that there is a lot more to him and Joan wanting to get away from here than them simply needing to start a new job. Quite apart from anything else, I want to know more about this island they're going to. I had asked Chris to look into it for me but he hasn't managed yet. Just what could draw two comfortable GPs to a remote place like that?'

Suzalinna shrugged. 'Beats me.'

'And another thing,' Cathy went on. 'It didn't pass my attention that the name of the room that Kenneth was murdered in was Skeln Suite. It all seems a little like too many coincidences for my liking.'

Cathy got up. 'Oh, I meant to ask you before, what was it you were talking to the chief inspector about earlier?'

'When, darling?'

'We were waiting to hear what was happening today and you and he walked in together. I thought you'd told him everything you knew already?'

'Oh, he was wanting more bloody details, Cath. Still harping on about the first day and us setting up the room.'

'Skeln Suite?'

'Yes, I told him actually that there was a funny miscommunication, I suppose you'd call it.'

Cathy looked up. 'What do you mean "miscommunication?"'

'Just that I didn't know who took out the bulb.'

Cathy cast her mind back to that fateful morning when they had discovered Kenneth's body. She recalled Suzalinna at the door to the room, her hand reaching around for the light switch. 'Of course! How could I have missed it?'

'Missed what? There's nothing exciting about it. We planned for that room to be in darkness but it was agreed that the light bulb would be removed just before we sent you in. We might have needed bits and pieces from that room during the morning and also, it was a hotel room. We couldn't start taking it to pieces and leaving it like that overnight.'

'Who removed the bulb then? When you flicked the switch the light didn't come on.'

'Well, I'll tell you exactly what I told the chief inspector and he looked bored to death when I said it too so I doubt it's of much interest. The answer is I don't know who took it. Either Duncan or Kenneth must have taken it away. My money's on Kenneth but the fact of the matter is we'll probably never know. And what does it matter anyway, Cathy? Who cares about a bloody light bulb when you've got two corpses to think about?'

34

Gus had known he had cancer now for almost eight months. He knew also that it was incurable and that with every passing month, he trod closer to death. Ageing had never bothered him. If anything, he had embraced the process. After all, he had won at life. He had met his soulmate and he had lived his days in companionship, doing a job he loved. But more than that he had found home. He wondered how many people could say that. Of course, he didn't mean the location, although that was very much part of it. Skeln had a magnetic pull for him, as it did Mary. He wasn't sure he believed in such things but sometimes he wondered if in a previous life he had lived there. Was that why it had all felt so familiar when he first arrived? As he had walked the tracks up to farms, the grassy lanes interspersed with tufts of sheep fleece and creeping juniper, he had known where he was. Home. When he wasn't on the island, and that had been only a handful of weeks in his forty years living there, he felt bereft. It was a yearning. A hunger to be back, so strong that on the ferry returning, he might find himself wiping his cheeks with his handkerchief and blowing his nose.

Getting old wasn't the issue. He had felt his body slowing

over the years, the aches and pains of his fifties and early sixties had been almost welcome. An indication that he had made it this far. The new symptoms were a source of growing understanding for his patients. With every stage in his life, his medical empathy had grown and his compassion for his patients increased. He watched his wife age also and rather than detract from her beauty, it only added to it. Each line on her face and greying hair, a record of their years together.

But death itself was a problem. Having to confront the realisation that life was finite and, if he was honest with himself, he could feel it, this was humbling indeed. He could feel life slowing ebbing away, like a receding tide. It was the most traumatic epiphany. He wondered if any of his patients had suffered it also. Had they looked death so squarely in the face and despised it for cheating them of more?

Oh, he knew he had led a wonderful and greatly fulfilling life. And yet, it was unfair. It was so deeply and tragically unfair. As he went about his daily rounds, tending to the islanders, counting the days until the new doctors would arrive and absolve him of his beloved duty, he seethed. His patients all knew now. Many didn't mention it out of respect. Still, he saw their sideways glance as they left the surgery. The look of pity was now one he knew only too well and it sickened him every time.

His main concern was always for her though. It had been so since the start. Mary wasn't like other women. He'd realised that very soon into their marriage. In years gone by, it would have been termed a 'fragile nature'. As descriptions went, it did pretty well. He had toyed with the idea of not telling her at all, or even explaining that the cancer wasn't that bad. But Mary would have seen through it and besides, he had never lied to his wife in all their years together. The last thing he wanted to do was to deceive her now. What sort of a parting gift would that be?

Still, though, he had tried to shield her. His symptoms had worsened. His chest became tighter and his breathing less easy. The cancer in his bones made him wince with pain at times, but in her company, he didn't complain and when the pain became too much to bear, he sat in his study praying for the relief sleep might offer him in a couple of hours that night.

Her nightmares had begun again. They had started after the couple had been to look at the island. That weekend had been terrible. He seemed nice enough. Charles, his name was, and the islanders would like him. They'd warm to her too, although she had been a little distant and shy. They had liked the place. She'd been to visit as a young girl and had always fancied coming back. It sounded like a bit of a spur of the moment thing. Neither of them would practice for more than ten years in reality because of their age but ten years was something and two doctors on the island, a great advantage. They had come to the surgery and he had gone over some things, the daily running of the practice and the layout of the farms and so on. Mary had cooked an evening meal for them all. She'd been bright and hospitable, as always but when they left, he knew it had upset her. It upset him also. The end of an era, the beginning of the end for him. Oh God, how would Mary cope? That night, she had suffered badly. And the dreams hadn't stopped since.

Now, if he managed to sleep himself, he was often woken by her calling out. He felt he was to blame. Anxiety of any sort brought it on and his illness and the inevitable changes ahead must plague her thoughts. It had been that way throughout their lives when anything worried her. Before he used to wake her by touching her shoulder. Sometimes that hadn't been enough and he'd wrap his arms around her waist, drawing her to him and holding her until she woke, dazed and bewildered, breathless always. But those days were long gone. Now, he was afraid of her flailing arms. Her legs, when they kicked and thrashed could catch his painful bones. Rather than wake her recently, he had shifted away to the safety of the other side of the bed. From there, he would call out her name. 'Mary. Just a dream. Mary, wake up. It's just a bad dream.'

Now, he hardly recognised his voice and the words were empty.

35

'I don't mind in the least, Cathy,' Charles said, pulling his tweed jacket about him and looking far more cheerful than he should.

She had just told him that Suzalinna and Duncan were planning to resume the course with the assessment and certification that afternoon. Duncan had apparently cleared it with the department and the chief inspector and it seemed that no one had any objections.

'Well,' Charles said, smiling. 'What is it I can do for you? You've not had much luck so far. Discovering two dead bodies isn't the nicest. Still, you're used to it. Well, more so than the rest of us. Have you come up with the solution yet? Which one of us is in the frame?' His eyes twinkled and Cathy felt rather sick.

'I wanted to ask you about Skeln.'

Charles's face fell. 'Oh? What about it?'

'It's just, well, forgive me for saying so, but it is a bold move.'

Charles nodded and his face relaxed. 'That's Joan for you. Always been headstrong. People think I'm the one in charge but it's her. Joan wears the trousers.'

Cathy smiled politely. 'I just wondered if there was a reason why you decided to make the move now and not earlier in your career?'

Charles shifted in his seat. 'Well, the advert only came up this year. The old boy on the island's decided to jack it in. Time to retire. Joan saw the announcement and couldn't get it out of her head.'

'But the urgency to go?' Cathy persisted. 'I know this course was very important to you. Your start date though, surely it could have been moved?'

Charles shrugged. 'Nice to have things settled.'

'Are you both still working at your old practice?'

The room was silent save the sound of the clock. Cathy knew immediately that she had hit a raw nerve. His face changed and his affable manner became defensive and wary.

'Southgate?' He asked. 'No. No. Decided to take a break before the big move.'

'I see. Southgate? That's in South Ayrshire, isn't it? You'd worked there for long?'

'Twenty years.' He shook his head. 'Look, what is all this?'

Cathy smiled apologetically. 'I'm sorry. It's not meant to be the third degree. I was just curious. Of course, now you'll hopefully get your certification and you won't have to change your plans about Skeln at all.'

Charles beamed. 'That's right. Joan'll be pleased as punch. Be nice to get this awful business cleared up before we go though. I can't say I relish the idea of going to the local police station for questioning about it later.'

'Is there even a station on Skeln?'

Charles chuckled. 'Don't think they have many crimes there. No, I believe the closest one's on the mainland. But what do you think, Cathy? Made any headway? Joan seems very impressed with you. We're pinning our hopes on you clearing the whole thing up by teatime. What are your thoughts on the chief inspector?'

Cathy blushed and rolled her eyes.

'Not impressed with the investigation so far? I don't blame you. Joan and I were saying much the same and I'm sure the rest are thinking it. Why put a policeman in the building last night if they weren't going to keep an eye on things? How can they have missed one of us sneaking around the corridors in the middle of the night? It doesn't look good.'

'I think they were downstairs,' Cathy said. 'The chief inspector had put a man at the door in the lobby. It was more to keep the conference suite monitored than anything else, I believe.'

'In case one of us disturbed the evidence, you mean? Those rooms have locks surely? Why not lock up and then have their man on guard in our corridor upstairs? We're all sleeping in the same wing, aren't we? I'm no criminal expert like yourself, but it does make more sense. One of us is dead and at least in part, it's due to their poor handling of the original case.'

Cathy grimaced. 'I agree. I don't suppose they were expecting a second murder though.'

'Well, none of us was but Joan and I have spoken about it, of course. We all have, I'm sure.'

'And?'

'It's pretty obvious why that poor young woman was killed last night. There is only one reason she could have been. She saw something on the first night, didn't she? The night Kenneth was killed.'

Cathy nodded. The same thought had occurred to her also. Martha had left the meal early. She had announced to the table that she was going up to bed. Cathy cursed herself for sleeping so deeply that night. Had she not, she might have been able to confirm one way or another if Martha had returned to the room.

But in some ways, it didn't matter. Martha had been seen in the lobby. It was much later on. Cathy wished she'd been on better terms with Martha that following day and that she had asked her what she had seen. It was the only explanation for her death, after all. She had seen someone behaving strangely that night. Perhaps at the time, she didn't think an awful lot about it but come morning when they discovered Kenneth in the scenario room, she must have realised that what she had witnessed was important.

'Well,' Charles continued. 'I suppose now, we'll all watch what we're saying in the group. Who knows, what we say as a passing remark might be misinterpreted and put us in danger too.'

'Have you and Joan any thoughts as to who might have done it?'

'None at all. As I say, we know why Martha was killed. She had to be silenced for what she saw. Maybe she spoke to the killer in private and asked what they'd been up to that night in the corridor. That put an end to that. As for Kenneth...'

Cathy waited.

Charles wrinkled his nose and sniffed loudly. 'I don't think any of us liked him, did we? Well, that's if we're being honest. That's not reason enough to kill, but he was a rather unpleasant character.'

'He was unfair I thought during the practical that afternoon.'

'With me, you mean? Water off a duck's back,' Charles blustered. 'No, that was long forgotten. In the evening, we were on better terms. He had a job to do. His way of asserting himself, I suppose. If it made him feel better about himself, so be it. I'm not easily ruffled or offended, Cathy. I can forgive and forget.'

Cathy thought that this was a wild exaggeration and if true, it was only possible as the other man was now dead. She'd seen how angry Charles was at being belittled by Kenneth in front of the rest of the group. No one could be that magnanimous. 'Had you and Joan discussed why he might have been targeted then?'

'Well, we've all be thinking about it, haven't we? The chief inspector asked too. Tricky... I wondered about that Jamie fellow. Rotten egg that one, and Kenneth certainly had it in for him, didn't he?'

'Joan mentioned that he had reminded you of someone. An old trainee, was it?'

Charles folded his arms. 'Oh, she said? Yes, as it happens, he did remind me of someone. Bit of a disaster that one. I knew he'd be tricky from the start. If you've done any training yourself, you'll know you get a bit of a hunch about them when they come.'

'I've not. I'd love to one day, but the opportunity hasn't arisen yet.'

'No, well you'll see. They turn up all smartly dressed and on the first couple of days, you know it's a bit of an act. By the second week, you have a fair idea if your hunch was correct.'

'The trainee Jamie reminded you of?'

'Sorry, yes. Well, a bit older he was. Think he'd done another degree first and changed over to medicine. Maybe he didn't get the grades to get in straight from school. Anyway, he was like that. Arrived with a notebook and was hanging on every word I said. I told Joan about him. He was one of my first trainee registrars and back then, I was a bit naive myself maybe. I told Joan I thought he was a good one. Jumpy and a bit worried about things, but sometimes that's not a bad thing. It shows they care, doesn't it? He'd always come in early and he'd offer to do more than was expected. That was when we were trying to get our records up to date. We were changing from paper to digital notes and it was a bit of a mess, all in all. Well, he didn't need to but he offered to come in and help on weekends. As I say, it was rather unexpected and I was pleased. Academically, you see, he wasn't that brilliant? But often you find that doesn't matter so much. It's the attitude that gets you places and I thought him conscientious.'

'What happened to him?'

'He passed his membership exam with a good deal of assistance from me and the other doctors at the practice. I wrote a letter in support of him. It was the following year I heard. We gave him a good reference leaving us and he headed down south. Somewhere in the north of England, I think.' Charles looked at Cathy. 'Didn't end well. Meticulous undoubtedly, but a little too much so with one of his young female patients, I'm afraid.'

Cathy gasped. It hadn't been what she was expecting.

Charles smiled at her reaction. 'No, not good. Weakness there, you see? A propensity to be easily led. I do not doubt that the young woman patient he got involved with led him on in some way. He was probably flattered. He was hardly a strapping lad. Forgot his principles though and lost his head. Then, there was no going back. Struck off, and rightly so.'

'What a waste.'

'Well, quite. Don't misunderstand me though. I'm not accusing Jamie of molestation or anything. I'm simply pointing out that he's weak-spirited. People like that can get led astray. Joan and I discussed it. If he did kill Kenneth, he'd not been the brains behind it. Someone, and perhaps this is a bit of a stretch, but some woman's put him up to it. And a man like Jamie wouldn't be able to say no.' Charles began to get up, and dusting his trousers down, he stood.

'Just one more thing,' Cathy said. 'I wondered if you or Joan had received a note?'

36

Charles's face turned an ugly shade of red. 'Note? A note?'

'A few of the group have. It seems that there's a poison pen at work. I had wondered if it was the murderer but I'm not entirely sure. Someone did a good deal of research on the group of medics staying here. Planning it must have begun a good while before we arrived.'

Charles shook his head forcibly. 'Nothing. No note. Where would it have been left? I don't know... I don't see–'

At that moment, Joan came in and joined them. 'Hope I'm not interrupting the pair of you?'

Charles barely acknowledged his wife as she sat down.

'I've just been talking with the rest of the group and what a coincidence! But what was it you were asking, Cathy?' Joan asked. 'I hope he's giving you the information you need to sort this mess out? He'll have told you that we have lost all trust in the chief inspector after that poor girl's death?'

Cathy nodded. 'He said. I was just asking about a note. Some of the other course participants had received unpleasant messages under their doors. I wondered if you'd suffered the same?'

Joan looked at Charles.

'Obviously, I said no,' he told his wife.

Joan looked back at Cathy. 'No, we haven't.'

'Suzalinna's one was in her room,' Cathy explained. 'So was Jamie's. I suspect Martha received one, although I can't be sure and I also think she picked up one that was meant for me. The person responsible for leaving them was quite busy.'

'Not us,' Charles repeated mechanically. 'Joan and I haven't had the pleasure of anything of that kind. Nasty little game. No, we've not had a thing.'

Although she knew they were lying, there was nothing Cathy could do. He and Joan had received one too and for whatever reason, they didn't want to admit it. Cathy wished she knew what it had said. Something probably about the sudden decision to quit their jobs in the practice Charles had worked at for twenty years. An unusual decision, especially given that they must surely be within touching distance of retirement themselves. Just what could it have been to make them want to leave the comfortable environment of inner-city medicine for the solitude of island life?

As she turned to leave, Cathy considered. She could call Chris again and ask him to look into the McKinleys' work. There couldn't be many practices called Southgate in Ayrshire, after all. But this she felt was a little unfair on poor Chris who had had a dreadful nightshift. The last thing he needed was her waking him and asking favours and he wasn't keen on helping as it was, he'd made that quite clear. He wanted Cathy to drop the whole thing and leave it to the police. But there was one person who would know more about Charles and that was someone she dreaded talking to.

'Oh, Joan?' Cathy said when she reached the door. 'You said just now that there had been a coincidence. There have been a few too many of those over the last few days. What were you referring to?'

'I wondered when you'd get round to me.' Ryan grinned. 'I notice I'm pretty much the last. Any reason for that? Am I the lowest down on your list of suspects and the least likely to kill?'

Cathy blushed. In truth, the reason she hadn't spoken to Ryan yet was because of exactly what he was doing now. He made her feel uncomfortable. She'd felt this way from the start about two people; Ryan and the hotel owner. But unlike Mr Faber who was bound by professional decorum to give her some space, Ryan had no such quibbles. He patted her knee now and she flinched. He noticed and his smile broadened.

'I thought you'd be more upset if I'm honest,' Cathy said, coldly. 'You and Martha got on better than most, didn't you?'

'Were you jealous? I did offer to walk you to your room on the first night if you'll remember.'

'Hardly, Ryan.'

'Just kidding with you, Cathy, but we could have had some fun. Yes, right enough, I liked the girl Martha. Seemed intelligent...'

But there was only so much of his bravado Cathy could stomach. 'Seemed intelligent? But surely you knew only too well? I believe you were at medical school together?'

He froze, but almost immediately corrected himself. 'You heard that, did you, Cathy? Well, you are living up to your excellent reputation, aren't you? And who told you that, might I ask?'

'Joan.'

'Joan? I don't see how...'

'You were dating Martha when you were a registrar at

Charles's practice. Joan didn't ever meet you but she's good with names. Charles must have mentioned it...'

'My God. Well, she must have some memory and we were only just talking now. Why didn't she mention it?'

Cathy shrugged.

'Well then, yes as it happens. I did know Martha before the course. I knew her very well. We kicked about together a bit at med school and dated during our registrar year. It fizzled out as these things do but...'

'But you seemed happy enough to see her again. Were you planning to take up where you left off?'

Ryan smirked. 'I wouldn't have said no. Nice hotel, nice to share it with someone pretty.'

'And Martha? How did she feel about seeing you again?'

'A lovely surprise she said.' He laughed and Cathy thought he was quite cruel.

'She seemed surprised when you walked in but I don't think she was pleased. Not at the beginning anyway. Nor was Charles, or Jamie, for that matter. You seem to have had a bit of negative effect on certain members of the group.'

Ryan lifted his hands in acceptance. 'Is that my fault?'

'You tell me. What was the difficulty between you and Jamie? I've still not worked that out. He seems to have a real concern about you. I'd say he was afraid.'

'Ridiculous.'

'You've locumed a bit over the years, haven't you?' Cathy asked. It was only a guess but it had to be true. 'It's pretty common for newly qualified doctors to move around after their registrar year. I did so myself although I never went that far. You were talking about it over the meal and mentioned what a bore some places could be. I know you've settled into a new practice now but that's a fairly recent move, isn't it? Before that, you locumed on and off a good deal over the years. I just wondered if you ever worked in Jamie's practice?'

He let out a sigh. 'My, Cathy, you are marvellous.'

'Ah,' she said with satisfaction. 'So that's it. I assume you heard pretty quickly about the dreadful accident? You heard about the child who had an anaphylactic shock?'

'Bit of a mess by the sounds of things. I only did a couple of days there but I heard. They were still talking about it eighteen months on and he was darting about like a frightened rabbit. Pathetic. And then, what a shock to find myself on the same emergency course as the one and only Jamie. What a hoot.'

'I don't think Jamie saw it that way. He received a note under the door when he first arrived. He thinks it was you who wrote it.'

It was the first time Cathy thought he behaved genuinely. 'Note? I haven't written any notes.'

'Have you received any?'

'No.' Again, he was undoubtedly telling the truth. 'What are you on about?'

'Why did you swap courses?' She asked, suddenly changing tack.

'Excuse me?'

'According to Duncan, you were meant to be on the previous resus course. These courses fill up fast and yet you managed to swap. Why did you change the date?'

'Well, not so I could blackmail Jamie, that's for sure, and not so I could bump off one of the instructors either if that's what you're getting at.'

'No,' Cathy said. 'Not because of that at all.'

He sighed. 'If you must know, I did hear that she'd be here.'

'Martha?'

'Yes. I suppose I wondered...'

'I see.'

'Look, there's no crime in wanting to see what happened to your old girlfriend, is there? I was curious. She was a bit different from all the others. She had something about her. Ambitious and a bit aloof. I suppose I liked that. I wanted to see if she was still an ice queen or if she might have thawed a bit.'

'And how did you find her.'

'Unreceptive, as it happens.'

'Did you meet her that evening then, on the first night? Was that why she was in the lobby?'

He nodded. 'If you must know, yes. But like I say, she wasn't interested in picking things up again. It was a pity. I was keen to stay on after the course and explore our friendship again.'

Cathy sighed. She was suddenly exhausted with all this talk. 'What about Charles and Joan?' She asked, feeling dispirited. She'd found out very little from either Jamie or Ryan other than to have her suspicions confirmed.

Ryan let out a low whistle. 'You want to know about them too, do you? Well, I guess we're all wondering why an out-of-date couple of fuddy-duddies are hoofing it off to some remote island. Makes you wonder if they're running away, doesn't it?'

Cathy didn't answer. She'd had enough of his teasing and his games.

Ryan leaned forward and smiled wickedly. 'Good old Drs McKinley. I bet they got a note under their door, did they?' When she didn't reply he shook his head. 'No, perhaps you're best to keep some secrets close to your chest but I have no such quibbles. I don't know what's caused their latest desire to up sticks but I can tell you this, Charles was in hot water not long after I left his practice.'

Cathy shifted in her seat.

'Yes,' he nodded, enjoying her attention, 'Charles was very good with his elderly patients...'

She raised her eyebrows but didn't speak.

'Apparently failed to declare a little gift that one of his old dears left him in her will,' Ryan said in a mock whisper. 'Now, I'm no expert in ethics, Cathy, but I do know right from wrong and GPs are not allowed to accept personal donations. I believe it was a lesson we were taught as registrars. Ironic given that Charles was my trainer and it was more than likely him who had to lecture me on the subject. All the while he was pocketing some rich lady's inheritance. Hypocrite.'

Cathy shook her head in disbelief.

'Don't believe me? Well, I'm sure if you were as enterprising a detective as I heard, you'd be able to find out yourself. Who knows what the old devil's been up to this time? Perhaps the same, perhaps not. He doesn't seem short of a bob or two, does he? I'm surprised he's not comfortable enough off to just retire on his ill-gotten gains now, but maybe Joan won't let him. She's an ambitious woman, that one. Maybe she has bigger plans still...'

37

Cathy's head was swimming following her conversation with Ryan. She licked her lips, still trying to compose herself. Whether or not what Ryan had said was true, it spoke volumes about his character. She'd be glad when this was over and she hoped never to see him again. What sort of a person would delight in such a thing and especially given he was close at one time with one of the murder victims?

She could just imagine his glee at seeing Jamie. How he must have enjoyed goading the poor nurse practitioner knowing that he had a hold over him. Charles, too, was in some ways at his mercy although that story still didn't seem right to Cathy. If Charles had embezzled money or whatever it was Ryan insinuated, he'd surely not want to go and work out his days on Skeln. Why not retire early and move abroad? People did it all the time. A quiet life in the sun. If what he had done was so bad, surely that would have been a safer option, and yet, here he was with his wife, doing a resuscitation course, hating every minute of it and dreading the prospect of going it alone. No, none of it made any sense. But more than anything, Cathy didn't like the way Ryan had revelled in it all.

'Horrible, just horrible,' she said to herself. But something was still unclear. Why had Ryan not received a note? It seemed that just about everyone else had. To most people, the fact might seem incriminating but although she was disgusted by his behaviour, she wasn't convinced. If anything, the note writer might direct attention away from themselves by pretending to receive an unpleasant letter. That would be the clever thing to do anyway. Who then had been lying? Who had acted outraged when in fact, they hadn't received one at all?

And then Cathy realised, of course, there was one person she had forgotten. One person she was still to speak to and had, up until now, passed under the radar. Duncan. After all, who other than Duncan, the long-suffering sidekick to Kenneth's unpleasant remarks, might wish the man dead? He, above all others, had been forced to listen to Kenneth's bragging and to watch his appalling teaching style. Not only that, but Kenneth, a strange and controlling man it seemed, had already done some research on his fellow instructors. Suzalinna's incident with Roderick had been dredged up. What then of Duncan? Had Kenneth found something out about him, and, if so, was it enough to kill for? It certainly seemed the most plausible theory yet. She'd need to check if Suzalinna's friend, Brodie, had managed to find out anything unusual about him.

But when Cathy spoke to Suzalinna, she was disappointed. Brodie had found nothing on the instructor at all. Duncan was a well-respected consultant paramedic. He had an excellent track record and no one had anything negative to report about him. Cathy felt irritable and dissatisfied. There had to be something. But perhaps he'd slip up talking to her and confess what the secret was. It was a long shot, but maybe it would do him good to get it off his chest. Maybe that, along with confessing to the double-murder too, she thought ruefully, but that was probably a push.

Cathy walked through the lobby, passing Andrea at reception, who looked, quite frankly, awful. She was leaning heavily on the reception desk and her face was pale and worried.

'I don't suppose you've seen Duncan?' Cathy asked.

Andrea looked up and smiled sadly. 'Not passed through while I've been here.' Her eyes flitted to the side and Cathy saw that they were being watched by a police officer who was positioned by the corridor to the scenario rooms.

'Can't have been an easy few days for the hotel staff,' Cathy said, lowering her voice. 'How are you and how's Mr Faber coping?'

Andrea shook her head slightly. 'Not good. It's been a strain. Mr Faber's a lovely man. Wants to do his best for everyone and I know he's trying to help the police but... Well, you can imagine, it's not easy having all of these people here. The reputation of the hotel rests on this being cleared up as tactfully as possible. Mr Faber's put a lot of work into the place. His heart and soul. He deserves it to do well.'

'Yes. I understand. He's lucky to have an employee who speaks so highly of him. You're clearly as dedicated to the work as he is. How long have you been here? Wasn't it only a couple of years?'

Andrea nodded. 'I trained in hospitality at university but I counted myself lucky to get this job. Good ones are hard to find. I've been on placements where the staffing situation is awful. People come and go for a good reason. Usually, because something's wrong at the top. Some hotel owners don't care about your training after you're working for them. They just set you your tasks and that's you. It can go on for years, doing the same things day in, day out and never progressing. But not Mr Faber. He actually cares. He wants my opinion on things and he listens to what I suggest. He encourages me to move up the career ladder. I see that as a sign of a good leader. Someone who helps others around them to succeed too.'

Cathy smiled at the girl's enthusiasm. 'And offering the hotel for this course?'

'Yes, well that's just so like him. He wants to help. Of course, he's a businessman first and foremost, but he supports local causes, he wants to put something back into the community.'

Cathy nodded. 'You mentioned Mr Faber wanting to help with our course in particular?'

'It was because of the accident. It affected him a good deal. His brother died. Mr Faber was driving. A terrible crash. I think he blames himself but that's madness. He was lucky to get out alive himself, by the sounds of things. If it hadn't been for the emergency services...'

'That was why he had hosted the resuscitation course in the first place, wasn't it? You mentioned it when I first arrived and said he was lucky to have walked away. I know it's a long shot but I don't suppose he knew any of the course participants or instructors before they came, did he?'

Andrea glanced again at the policeman still standing unobtrusively in the corner of the lobby. 'I think you'd have to ask him... I don't... No, I couldn't say for sure...'

Cathy wondered if the girl had realised the implication of her boss knowing someone beforehand. Was she taking her loyalty to Mr Faber a step further and protecting him from suspicion? Cathy couldn't be sure, but it was clear that Andrea wasn't going to say anything else and when the telephone rang, she smiled in relief at Cathy and picked it up signalling the end of their discussion.

Cathy wandered through the lobby thinking over what had

been said. The circular table still held its offering of thistles and roses in an enormous display but it looked far less succulent and upright than a few days before. The rose heads bowed over the edge of the bowl in which they had been arranged and the thistles looked dusty and sad.

Climbing the stairs to the corridor from which all the bedrooms led off, she wondered if the chief inspector was questioning Duncan and if that was why he was nowhere to be seen, but then the whole place had gone a bit quiet. Where was everyone?

She had expected a police presence outside or around Martha's door, but the corridor was empty and the door shut. Cathy had seen Duncan going into his room the previous night and knew which one was his. She stood at the door feeling a little anxious and not knowing how she should approach the conversation. Finally, she summoned her courage and knocked. Nothing.

Cathy looked up and down the corridor again and then realised where they must all be. Duncan and Suzalinna had, of course, been planning on doing a brief teaching session that morning to allow the course participants who wanted it to gain their certification. They must have all congregated in one of the scenario rooms. She hovered in the corridor wondering what she should do. And then, impulsively, she tried the handle to Duncan's room. It turned but the door didn't open. Cathy stepped back, her hands shaking. She looked up and down the corridor once more but she was completely alone. If only she could get inside the room, she might find the note that must surely have been posted under Duncan's door. Cathy felt quite certain now that he had received a nasty message also. No one was squeaky-clean. Duncan had to have something in his past.

Cathy quickly descended the stairs once more, her feet nimble and quiet on the carpeted floors. In the lobby, she was surprised to see that Andrea was no longer at reception, but she heard a door opening and the sound of voices filtered through.

'Ah, thank you, Andrea. Just down there, if you don't mind.'

She was taking them refreshments.

Cathy saw the policeman watching her. She stood uncertainly but her luck was in because, at that moment, the chief inspector appeared. 'Dr Moreland?'

Cathy nodded. 'Yes, can I help?'

'Not taking part in the rest of the course?'

Her heart was hammering in her throat. 'I thought it wasn't the right time,' she said. 'Were you needing to talk to me?'

'Not just yet, but soon. I'm talking to Dr Oliver just now.' He turned to the young police constable who was still standing in the hall. 'Get onto the station and see if there's anything else back on the post-mortem for me, will you? I think we're about ready to wrap up things with the crime scene but I need to be sure if I'm to free up the rooms.'

The young police officer nodded and going to the front door, spoke into his radio. The thing crackled and he grimaced. 'Interference's bad here. I'll just go outside.'

The chief inspector nodded and turned once more to Cathy who was holding on to the reception desk.

'Ten minutes, Dr Moreland, and then I'll have a word if I may?'

Cathy nodded and smiled. 'Ten minutes. I'll hang around and wait.'

He disappeared and glancing about her, Cathy knew she'd have to be quick. She skirted the reception area and nipped behind the desk. Her eyes flitted over the books and computer screen but it was the keys she was after. Duncan's room was number twenty-one. The keys jangled as she tried to slide the thin metal over the hook. If she wasn't quick, she'd be seen. She heard a door opening in the conference suite and launched herself around the side of the desk again, to where she should be standing.

When Andrea appeared, she was standing by the circular table looking at a pile of magazines that rested there. But gripped tightly in the palm of her hand was the key to Duncan's room.

38

Cathy knew she was taking a dreadful risk. The chief inspector would be looking for her in ten minutes and if for any reason, Duncan returned to his room, she'd be discovered. No explanation would suffice. There was no reason for her to be in there other than snooping.

Much to her relief though, the corridor upstairs was still deserted. She walked quickly, trying to calm her breathing and, if anyone did suddenly open a door, appear confident. The key was tricky. Her hands, despite her best efforts, wouldn't do as she told them and the tip of the metal repeatedly slid on the lock.

Once inside, she stood with her back to the door, her chest rising and falling in gasps. But she had to be quick. Frantically, she looked around the room. Where should she start? In reality, she was looking for two things. The light bulb that had been mysteriously removed from the scenario room. It might well incriminate Duncan if she found it but more importantly, she wanted to find a note. But where would he put it? The first place of course was the bin. It had been where she had herself instinctively put Suzalinna's letter so it made sense to look there.

The room was set out in the same fashion as her own but a mirror image as it was on the other side of the corridor. The bin would be under the dressing table. But Cathy was disappointed when she looked. In the bin, under some cellophane wrapping and a small cardboard tray were only a few receipts and a chocolate wrapper. Where next?

By his bed, Duncan had laid out some of his clothes. Cathy began to gently lift these, but it was a silly place to look. Perhaps his bag would be a better option or even the drawer to the small bedside table. Cathy looked here first. It was empty save a Bible. His bag would be more awkward. It was a loose canvas knapsack and Cathy had to reach right inside and remove almost the whole contents to be thoroughly sure. With every item of clothing or personal belonging she brought out, the deeper her despair grew. It was a daft idea really, to think he'd put something like that in his bag, anyway.

Cathy stood now in the centre of the room. She had to think clearly. Where would he put a note? She tried to put herself in Duncan's position. He'd just read a vindictive letter. What then would he do? Cathy looked up. The window? Might he tear it up and toss it out? It was certainly a possibility. If he had, she'd have little luck in finding the pieces on the ground below. The previous night had been windy and surely nothing would be left. Cautiously, she slid open the latch and lifted the heavy frame. Then, leaning out, she peered down. Below the window was a bush but there was no obvious sign of scraps of paper. Further disheartened, Cathy closed the window. She could check under the window later, of course, but what if she'd been wrong. Maybe there had been no letter at all. Perhaps Duncan did have nothing to hide. Or, there was the opposite theory that had to be addressed. Maybe he was the poison pen himself and had obviously not sent himself a note. Cathy wondered if she'd got it all wrong. She had assumed that the murderer and poison pen were one and the same, but maybe they were different people.

Before she left Duncan's room empty-handed, she thought she'd better check the bathroom. Obviously if he'd done the same as her and flushed his note down the toilet, there'd be nothing to show of it, but for completeness, she should look.

The bathroom was as orderly as his bedroom with his toiletries neatly lined up on the glass shelf. She wasn't sure what made her do it, but without thinking, she lifted his toiletry bag. The fan in the bathroom hummed. It drowned out the sound of a key turning and the approaching footsteps.

'Just what the hell are you doing?'

39

'How long?' Cathy asked.

She and Duncan sat opposite one another on the twin beds. He said he'd come up to his room to collect something, but Cathy wondered if he had a bit of a sixth sense about things. She did herself. After all, what else had made her look in his bag?

Duncan sighed. 'It's been on and off for probably fifteen years. Awful, I know. I relapsed about six months ago. It's been a struggle since. Not that it interfered with work, but I know I have that in me, the ability to self-destruct. It's as if my thumb's poised and hovering over the button constantly.'

'This course can't have been easy.'

Duncan looked skyward. 'Not easy, no, but it was manageable. Since the police arrived, I've struggled more probably.'

Cathy held up the packet of pills. Printed on the silver foil was the word Antabuse. Disulfiram, its other name, was a treatment commonly used in conjunction with counselling for recovering alcoholics. It was meant to act as a strong deterrent as drinking any ethanol within a day or so of taking a tablet, would make the person incredibly unwell.

'It's worked to a point,' Duncan said. 'I knew the course would be a bit of a test as it was. I've not had a drink, obviously, but the temptation hasn't gone. I suppose I'm disappointed in myself. I thought I'd be over this by now at my age.'

'I'm guessing that having Kenneth sitting beside you at meals and in the evening can't have helped?'

Duncan smiled. 'Not a great help, no.'

'He knew?'

'He did. I'm not sure how, but I did feel a little embittered. I took the role of instructor in good faith and hoped to make a difference. As soon as I met Kenneth though, I knew it would be tricky.'

'It was almost as if he was taunting you then? The way he was drinking in front of you and I even heard him asking you to order him a whisky.'

'A little childish of him, yes. But I think he was like that. It's no real secret that I had a problem although I'd say, few people probably know about it now. I have, to a degree, more self-control than I used to when I was younger but it doesn't leave you and the Antabuse was a backup for this weekend.'

'I suspect Kenneth had issues with alcohol himself.'

'Yes.'

'But he'd not yet come to the point of recognising or admitting it.'

'No.'

They sat in silence for some moments.

'I am sorry to have been in here,' Cathy said, suddenly embarrassed. 'I was looking for something other than this,' she said, touching the pill packet. And, to Duncan's raised eyebrows, she continued, 'A few people on the course have received nasty letters. I wondered if you had...'

He got up and felt in his back pocket. 'Like this?' He asked, withdrawing a crumpled scrap.

Cathy took it and unfolded the paper. '*Drunken bastard! Not fit to practice.*'

'Oh dear.' Cathy sighed.

'Quite. Well, someone knew other than Kenneth, anyway. I don't know what they hoped to achieve putting the note here. I suppose like you, they managed to get a key and...'

But Cathy had stopped listening. 'I wonder,' she said. 'Which bed did Jamie sleep in that first night?'

'Excuse me?'

Cathy looked at Duncan as if seeing him for the first time. 'Sorry, Duncan, and I'm sorry for coming in here and doing what I did.' She got up. 'I need to have a word with Jamie, and then, I think, the chief inspector. It's the only thing that makes sense and how stupidly simple if it's true. But I still need to find out why.'

40

G us moved across his consulting room. His steps were more careful than they used to be and his breathing laboured. That morning, he had been going through his things. The building needed a good tidy up before the new doctors took over. Mary had offered to come down to help, but he preferred to do it alone and she understood without him needing to explain. All those years, all those memories. It would be so hard to say goodbye.

He looked about the small room that had been the heart of his vocation. Those magnolia walls, a little faded perhaps and the paintwork chipped in places, but a good place to have been. A happy place. He had taken the wall posters down already and rolled them up in case the new doctors had use for them. His paintings had been taken home last week too, just a couple that a local artist had done. The woman who had painted them had caught the light of the sea by the harbour beautifully and he couldn't say no when he saw them for sale some fifteen years back.

On his desk, a photograph of Mary. She must have been in her forties when he had taken it. Her hair had been swept across her face by the wind and she smiled at him. Her eyes were squinting, blinded by the sun, so full of love. Behind her was the shore just along from their house, the cove where, for the last forty years of him knowing her, she had swum every summer. He reflected on it now. It was one thing Mary had always kept back, something she had done alone. Everything else was together, but the sea was hers. When they started getting serious about one another, he had suggested he come to keep her company. Gus wasn't a strong swimmer but, in his mind, it was safer not to go alone. But she had been adamant. She didn't need or want him there. She wasn't rude but she was quite clear about it.

After her mother explained about the drowning at Sandeels, he did wonder if it was some kind of ritualistic process she had to go through, a way of being near to her friend, Becca, who had died all those years ago. Certainly, they never went to Sandeels, even on their walks around the island together, she would tug at his sleeve. 'Not that way, let's go to Craignuir Sands instead. It's more sheltered down there.' He couldn't blame her for that.

He picked up the photograph and studied it, going over every bit of his wife's face. It would stay. He'd pack up the rest but the photograph would be the last thing, the final thing to go in his box that last day before handing over the reins. And what would they make of his little practice, Gus wondered. It certainly wasn't a patch on what they had probably known previously.

Other practices had long since moved on with computer data recording. They had computer systems and appointment structures. On Skeln, things were rather different. What with power cuts in the winter and a general distrust of anything electronic, he had kept to paper notes. As for appointments, well, he saw people when they needed to be seen. People couldn't help being unwell outside the nine-to-five that many doctors worked. No, to the new doctors, that might well come as a bit of a shock to the system.

Gus continued through the small building, past the little toilet cubicle and the store cupboard and through to the back room. Here there was line after line of dusky pink folders. Gus picked up a couple and flipped through the pages. He knew all of these people as if they were his family. More often than not, the notes would stay here and he'd only remember to document his consultations much later. It was all committed to memory. Folk didn't like you to be scribbling in their notes while talking to them anyway. When he had seen the oncologist on the mainland he had been almost unable to meet Gus's eye he was so intent on typing up his examination findings before the next one came in. Not, in his opinion, a good way to deal with people and the people of Skeln were all rather stuck in their ways.

Back in his consulting room, he looked at the half-filled cardboard box. He had emptied his drawers knowing that it would be too painful to do so nearer the time. In the box were the trinkets and bits that he had brought to work over the years. He reached in and picked out a jar and smiled. Inside the jar was a collection of shells. Common and tatty to some, but precious to him. Each held a memory. A memory of a walk with Mary. It had been something she had started when they first began dating, a 'little reminder of me,' she had said the first time, pressing the ridged cone of translucent purple into his palm. He hadn't needed a reminder he said, but he kept it all the same, along with all the others. Now, many walks ended with a shell. He helped her look for them and still enjoyed her childlike delight at finding a special one, one that was a little different or had a pretty pattern. Something to remember her by. A reminder of his wife, his marriage, of his whole life.

Gus sighed and replaced the jar in the cardboard box. He'd find a good place for them at home, perhaps in his office, maybe on his desk. He looked along the shelves just above his desk. Some old textbooks were still lined there. Long since forgotten, although when he first arrived on the island, they were regularly thumbed. No point in keeping them himself, he thought. He'd leave them for the new GPs. There were more up-to-date versions but these were still good editions. He had no use for anything of that kind now and keeping hold of them was sentimental nonsense.

Gus thought of the two doctors who, in a matter of weeks now, would replace him. They had seemed nice enough but how would the islanders take to the change? When they had come over to visit earlier in the year, Gus had introduced them to old Ms Keith who would undoubtedly be one of the hardest to please. She'd still not forgiven him for leaving the island for a short holiday with Mary and employing a locum, and that was five years ago now.

Gus thought of that holiday, a much-needed break, and shuddered. What a dreadful thing to return to. Going had been a mistake in some ways, even he had to admit that. Not that he could have changed any of the appalling events but he might have been able to offer the family of the poor man a little more comfort than the locum doctor standing in for him. Probably hadn't come across anything of the kind before. Still, that was the danger of not knowing the island and its waters. The place had seen disaster before with ships being lost and of course, the drowning at Sandeels, but the accident, while he was away, could not have been foreseen by anyone, no matter what Ms Keith said. Admittedly, the boy had been a fool but no one could have known what might happen to him.

After that tragedy, there had been a petition to get a lifeboat stationed on the island permanently. The crossing was treacherous, after all. No one could deny it. But in the end, following an enquiry, it was decided that the fault had been with the boy himself. What business had he in the sea on that side of the island anyway where the waves were unpredictable and the currents strong?

The answer was, of course, that he had come across from Oban. A day trip with a group of youths. The big waves on Scarnaig Bay were well known. Few people came to visit Skeln but if they did, they were nature-lovers or surfers. A temperate climate during the summer and prevailing south-westerly winds from the Atlantic made it ideal. Sadly, that day had not been so perfect for the surfer or for the people who tried to rescue him. There had been a big enquiry into that also. Gus heard from some of the locals who had watched in horror from the shore as the dreadful events unfolded. They'd tried to send out a lifeboat but couldn't reach him. Miraculously, he had managed to get clear of the water though. Dragged himself onto the rocks and had foolishly begun to climb up to get further from the frothing sea. Had he stayed where he was, they might have picked him up when the wind calmed, but they couldn't and a helicopter was scrambled.

What a din it had made they said and the sand had blown up in a dust storm all around them, making them turn their backs to the scene. Gus heard that there had been a problem with the winch line and though usually a man would go down and collect a casualty, instead they lowered the rope and instructed the lad to slip it over his shoulders. Unfortunately, it hadn't gone to plan and for whatever reason, he hadn't secured himself properly. Watched by the horrified crowd the boy had been lifted safely from the rocks, only then to slide from his harness, smashing down heavily on them again. He was killed outright.

Gus closed his eyes in recollection of the aftermath on his return. Many had been traumatised watching it, none more so than the poor locum doctor who had had to pronounce the young man dead and break the news by telephone to his family on the mainland. Terrible.

Gus moved around his desk and collected his box. At least he'd made a good start on clearing things though. He'd do the rest over the following week. Turning off the light, he looked back at his consulting room. He hoped the new doctors would love Skeln as much as he had. He hoped they were prepared also for all that it had. It could be an idyllic place, but cruel also. A place of great joy, but potential tragedy also. That had been more than proved over the years.

41

The group was gathered in the Islay Suite. Suzalinna had been going over a couple of things before the informal assessment planned for later that day. By the window, Jamie sat a little apart and to the far right of him, Charles and Joan. Ryan had decided to join them which was a surprise. Although, having announced loudly earlier that he didn't care anymore whether he had his certificate or not, he apparently hadn't wanted to miss out on the fun. Duncan nodded at Cathy as she entered the room.

'Just going through neck stabilisation, Cathy, come and take a seat with us.'

She smiled. Having taken a call from Chris, she had gone directly to the chief inspector. He had been very interested in what she had had to say. In truth, she was a little disappointed not to have had a chance to speak to Jamie alone, but she now had all the evidence she needed and as everyone was here, there seemed no better time.

'Sorry to come in late,' she said quietly and cleared her throat.

Suzalinna looked sharply at her, perhaps knowing that she had something to say. 'Cath?'

'I didn't mean to intrude on your teaching, Suz, Duncan, but I thought I should at least explain a few things. The chief inspector is just about to leave. I've spoken with him and explained. Soon we will all be free to go.'

There was a murmur of surprise from the group.

It was Ryan who spoke first. 'Free to go? Hasn't he worked it out then? I thought the idea was that the chief inspector would finish interviewing all of us and then to save chasing halfway across the country again, arrest the person responsible. I think we're all quite aware that the killer must be in this room. Gives me the creeps but it is rather fun.' He looked around the group, a horrible smirk on his face. 'But why give them a chance to get away?' he asked, turning to Cathy once more.

Cathy nodded. 'Yes, I see what you mean. It does seem a little strange, perhaps, but the murderer won't escape justice, that I can promise.'

The door opened and the chief inspector came into the room. He looked around the group, his eyes finally resting on Cathy. There was an understanding and he nodded.

'I must admit I was a little thrown off course so to speak,' Cathy began faltering over her words. 'Kenneth was universally disliked by just about all of us. An unpleasant man, if you'll excuse me speaking ill of the dead, but it's true all the same. He had offered his services to the department, organising and running these emergency courses for years. I think more than it being a service to the wider medical world, he saw it as an opportunity to boost his ego.' She smiled. 'Perhaps I'm being a bit mean in saying that but when someone goes on and on about how wonderful they are and how skilled in their profession, it does ring alarm bells, for me anyway.'

'I never thought he was anything near as great as he made out.' Ryan laughed. 'I'm not surprised by your little revelation at all. Empty cans always make the loudest noise, after all. I can see him being a pain in the butt to work with. He liked a few too many drinks too.'

Cathy nodded. 'He did indeed. Judging by some of the telltale signs, he was a longstanding alcoholic.'

Ryan snorted in disgust.

'You've already made your feelings quite clear on the subject,' Duncan said suddenly.

All eyes turned to him. Perhaps he regretted not pulling Ryan up on his views that first night at the meal; maybe this was his chance to set things straight. 'God knows, I feel sorry for your patients if you're so lacking in empathy,' Duncan said. 'I thought we were here to help, not judge.'

Ryan smirked. 'I noticed you were sticking safely to the water. Recovering, are we? I've hit a raw nerve. What are the chances of two instructors having zero self-control? I'm wondering now about the third...'

Everyone looked at Suzalinna but she wasn't going to be patronised and she stared back at Ryan, her eyes cool. 'I've nothing to hide, Dr Oliver. What did you just say about empty cans? I think we've heard your voice an awful lot today.'

Ryan snorted. 'Reminds me of school.'

With that settled, the group returned their attention to Cathy once more. 'Yes, well, none of this is pleasant and I apologise for that,' she said. 'But Ryan is right to a certain extent. We all have our demons.' She looked around the room. 'In reality, every one of us came to this course with something from our past that we'd rather wasn't known. None of us could have predicted that while here, each of our secrets, each little smudge on our career, might be exposed. I think that before this course began, perhaps many months back, someone did a good deal of research into this group. And then, when we arrived, we had a nasty surprise waiting for us. Well, some of us at least.'

The room was silent and Cathy took a deep breath. She reached into her pocket. 'Duncan gave me this just an hour ago. A letter. A vicious note that was left in his room intimating that someone knew about his past. My dearest friend, Suzalinna. She had one also. I'll not go into what her one said, it's not relevant, but it was of the same ilk. Jamie, you also–'

'But I know who left mine.' He turned and glared at Ryan.

'Hold that thought, Jamie. I want to come back to it,' Cathy said. She turned to Joan and Charles. 'I think each of us received a note. Kenneth had one and while I haven't seen it, I can guess what it said. Martha also. And I did too, although it was Martha who read it. It accused me of something quite awful but there was some truth in what it said, hence why Martha's attitude to me changed after she'd been up to our room.'

Joan shifted in her seat. Her hands had been pressed into her lap and she clasped and unclasped them. 'Well, Charles and I didn't have a thing...'

Cathy shook her head but she didn't contradict the older woman. She turned to the rest of the group. 'Ryan, you didn't receive a note?'

He was lapsed back in his chair and raised his hands in a gesture of defeat. 'Sorry to disappoint. I wish in some ways I had. I feel a little hurt that no one bothered to scrutinise my past and I'm sure there would be so many things to dig up.'

Charles coughed. 'There would. You were a competent trainee but your moralities were always in question.'

'Utter hypocrisy!' Ryan guffawed. 'Tell us about the undeclared inheritance money, Charles. I'd not be surprised if you'd done the same again, hence the desperate move to Skeln.'

Cathy couldn't allow this to go on any longer. It was turning into a farce. She cleared her throat. 'The tiny island of Skeln seems to have been at the centre of things, funnily enough. Did anyone notice that the room Kenneth was killed in was called Skeln Suite? But I'll come back to that too. I did wonder for a while if the note writer and the killer were one and the same. Someone had an axe to grind about fitness to practice but then, as I say, Kenneth had rubbed so many of us up the wrong way, I thought each of us had a reason to wish him dead. Martha's fate also seemed sealed because she had observed Kenneth's killer loitering in the corridor that evening. That was what I thought anyway.'

She took a deep breath. 'I think though, I was quite wrong on both counts. Kenneth's murder was planned carefully. It wasn't a spur of the moment thing caused by his bad attitude that day. Martha's death too, well, I had the feeling that there was something more to it than just her seeing something she shouldn't. And what would she have seen? Why would anyone, even the killer, be hanging around the corridor to the scenario rooms. If they did intend to murder Kenneth later that night, what purpose did they have down there?'

Everyone stared at Cathy and she rubbed her forehead trying to clear her thoughts. 'But there was some preparation required. Suzalinna,' she said, turning to her friend. 'That scenario room had been laid out ready with the resus bag and dummy. There was something that worried you about it though, do you remember?'

Suzalinna nodded. 'You mean the light? But, Cath, it was stupid.'

Cathy turned to the chief inspector. 'That room was always intended to have a "lights-out" element to it. It was meant to make it trickier for the course participants, one of Kenneth's little schemes to test our competence. The thing was, there was one final thing that needed to be done before the group went into the room. The instructors had set it all up the day before but knowing that they'd need to check it one last time, they didn't remove the light bulb. That was the last thing that had to be done. Suzalinna, in her anger at being kept waiting, forgot about it. She flicked the light switch without thinking and when it didn't come on, she sent me, Martha and Joan in.'

'To make that dreadful discovery,' Suzalinna said, unhappily. 'I'm sorry for that.'

'But who removed the light bulb?' Charles asked.

'The killer, of course, after they had murdered Kenneth the previous night. They couldn't murder him in the dark, after all, could they? They removed the light bulb and set the room up like a scenario purely out of spite. A fitting end for the resuscitation instructor but a dreadful discovery for all of us. I think though, that was part of it also. We deserved to be punished too and finding him lying there will certainly stay with me for a long time. They chose to kill him in such a cruel manner. Using a laryngeal mask to essentially suffocate him to death. Horrible.'

'But how could they physically do it? He was a big guy. Why didn't he put up a fight?' Suzalinna asked.

'It can't have been too hard to lure him into the corridor perhaps on the pretext of checking something in one of the rooms. He was very drunk and all it would have taken would be a knock to the head to silence him. Perhaps a mild tranquilliser in his drink that evening even. Martha's killing was planned also and yet again, the killer chose a very particular way to end her life too. She could have been far more easily stabbed with a knife but no, they chose a wide-bore chest needle. Very clinical. Very medical.'

The room was still.

'So, it was one of us,' Suzalinna said. 'Who?'

Cathy turned to Joan. 'I'm sorry to do this in front of everyone, but your story has to be heard. I said before that the tiny island of Skeln was at the very heart of this crime. Joan, you've kept your dreadful secret, even from your husband, for long enough. Don't you think it's time to let it go?'

42

Joan looked wildly from Cathy to Charles.

'What is all this, Joan?' Charles asked. 'Tell her she's wrong. Tell her she has it muddled.'

Joan covered her face with her hands. Her whole body was trembling.

'What the hell are you trying to insinuate?' he barked at Cathy. 'My wife! How dare you even suggest it?'

But he was interrupted by a dreadful moan. 'Oh, for God's sake, Charles!' Joan wailed. 'Please, for once in your life, just listen.' She looked up at Cathy, her eyes haunted. 'I'll talk now. I'll tell my story. You're right. I've kept it a secret long enough.'

The rest of the group resettled, shifting so that now Joan was the focus of their attention. Cathy noticed that the door to the room had opened slightly, she saw Mr Faber look in, but seeing the chief inspector standing only a metre or so away, he quietly closed it once more, perhaps realising that it was a bad time.

Cathy nodded for Joan to begin. 'Please take your time, Joan. The story begins a long time ago, doesn't it? A trip, a special family holiday?'

Joan nodded. 'Yes, that's right. Although how you know, I don't understand. I went to the island of Skeln.'

The rest of the group sat mesmerised, and none more so than her husband who despite being married to her, had never before heard her speak of that wonderful windswept summer, of deep friendships forged but the cruelty of fear and jealousy that came with them.

'I don't even know if she recognised me when Charles and I went back,' Joan finally said, tears now streaming down her cheeks. 'I loved her, in a way, not romantically, of course, but it's so hard to explain. I've tried to analyse it since. I know we were just girls but she altered me in a way. She was like no one I had ever met before, or since. Her hair was like the wind. She had the sea running through her veins. I wanted to be her, to be with her. I didn't want to leave that place, not ever and in a way, I never did. It's been in my heart all these years. How could I get over that? No one could. I was just a child but I had lived an adult understanding. I had fallen in love and I had died too, all in the space of two weeks. It was like discovering myself. It was wonderful and liberating. But then, it was taken away.'

'Did you hear about the rumours afterwards?' Cathy asked. It was the first time she had spoken since Joan began and her voice sounded strained. She had been as affected by the woman's story as anyone in the room. A tale of desire, attachment and ultimately, betrayal. It was so hard to hear.

'The police spoke to my parents but nothing more was done. No one could prove anything. A girl was dead but when we left the island, we pretended it hadn't happened. You've no idea how it ate away at me. All these years I thought of her and wondered...'

'I think it shaped your life a good deal,' Cathy agreed. 'And in a good way also. You became a doctor, didn't you? Having experienced such a traumatic event, you wanted to atone, didn't you? You wanted to make up for what had happened that day?'

Joan nodded. 'You word it so well. Yes. The job became a self-sacrifice of sorts, I suppose. I enjoyed it, of course, but I saw it as an offering to make sure it hadn't been in vain. It was for her, you see? I did it for her. Becca.'

Cathy sighed. 'And then you saw the advert.'

Joan nodded. 'It changed everything. A calling. It was meant to be. I was meant to go back there, you see that, don't you? The island wanted me home. I had begun to wonder if it would be in this lifetime or the next, but this was my summons. I knew I had to go.'

Cathy grimaced. 'But the only way you could go was by attending this course. It became an obsession of sorts. And once you were here, I imagine it must have been quite a shock to see the scenario room named after "your" island. Fate again? Maybe, maybe not. But not only that, you met someone else who had been to the island also.'

Joan nodded enthusiastically. 'I could have spoken to her for hours about it. Martha had been more recently than me, you see? She'd worked there as a locum. She could remember the beaches and the paths, the houses and...'

But Cathy interrupted. 'Oddly though, she wasn't as enthusiastic as you?'

Joan shrugged. 'She seemed to want to change the subject and then, she went up to bed early. I thought it was rude, but each to their own. She wasn't a free spirit, perhaps. She didn't fall in love with it like me. In a way, I was glad it hadn't impacted her in the same way. It made it more specially mine.'

Cathy shook her head. 'I don't think it was as simple as that, Joan, was it? Martha's reaction was for a very different reason.'

Joan looked confused. 'I don't understand...'

'Skeln had witnessed the tragedy you described. The

drowning of a young girl, a girl belonging to the island who despite knowing the dangers of the water surrounding the island, had swum out there. Whether or not her death was ultimately at another's hands, might never be proven. It was too long ago. But the island suffered more than one heartbreak...'

The room was still, save the ticking of the clock on the wall. Cathy shook her head. What she was about to reveal was shocking, to say the least. 'The internet connection is poor here otherwise I'd have done the research myself. I regret that. Martha's life might not have been curtailed so cruelly if I had known.'

Still, no one spoke.

'There was another accident on Skeln. It happened some years after the one Joan described. This time, it wasn't a drowning though. A group of young lads visited the island from the mainland. A day trip to catch some surf, although they hadn't realised how unpredictable the tides could be. One boy got into difficulties. Some of the islanders watched but couldn't help him. Any boat would have been smashed against the rocks.' Cathy paused. 'The boy managed to haul himself up though apparently and sat on the edge of the cliffs waiting to be saved. Someone had called the emergency services and a helicopter was scrambled. But the rescue didn't go to plan...'

From the lobby, there was an excruciating scream. They all turned to look. Mr Faber had been standing at the doorway and his face was frozen like a mask. Slowly he turned from them. The chief inspector opened the door wide.

Her small frame had crumpled to the plush tartan carpet. Her skirt was rumpled and her face twisted in an agony of pain. Andrea, the girl from reception, lay sobbing. It was over.

43

The dawn light woke him, at least he thought that was what it had been. The touch of creamy-yellow sunlight brushing the curtains and shyly filtering into the room. Gus lay for some minutes assessing how his body felt. He seemed to spend most of his waking moments going through this process. His back had been the issue yesterday but the long-acting pain-relief had at least allowed him some rest. He shifted his weight and winced. The alarm clock read 5.30. Today was his last day.

The new doctors had come across yesterday evening and seemed a little nervous but they'd settle fine. The island would welcome them and they'd soon feel their way into things as he had done all those years before.

Turning over was not an easy task. He groaned and stretched out a hand. The other side of the bed was empty. Thinking that he had missed hearing her get up to go to the lavatory, he lay there thinking. His last day as a doctor on Skeln. How odd to think of it, but he had served his time and he'd been useful for the most part. He hoped he'd be remembered fondly as often old doctors were, his patients lamenting the loss of a 'good 'un' and perhaps complaining about the way medical matters were managed since.

He allowed his hand to caress Mary's side of the bed. She had been his rock throughout all of this.

The bed felt cold. So different from her warm softness, the loose lovely folds that age had bestowed her. He lay there, his breathing laboured but his heart full as he thought of his beloved wife, so fragile and perfect. How he wished it could have been the other way about.

Why was the bed cold?

Gus sat up, now concerned. Where was she? Where was Mary?

Blinking, he reached for his spectacles on the bedside table and then, he saw. It was addressed by a hand he knew so well, and yet, how well could you know anyone?

Dearest Gus,

You promised you'd never leave me and I believe you meant it. How could I allow you to break your word? I think you knew the truth about Becca all along, didn't you? She left me. She wanted to be with that girl, Joan. I don't know what came over me that day, Gus. It was a madness I'll never forget. And yet, I believe you knew all along and still loved me. What did I do to deserve you, my angel? Forgive me, my love.

I am forever yours, Mary.

They found her clothes in a neatly folded bundle at Sandeels Bay just as the sun came up on that side of the island properly. The locals said she must have walked out into the sea knowing that her husband had little time on this earth and perhaps they were right.

44

'I still don't see why she had to kill Martha though,' Suzalinna said stubbornly once things had calmed down. 'I mean, I can see her point about Kenneth. His poor decision about winching that boy led to his death. No wonder Andrea couldn't forgive him. Her brother died unnecessarily. He had managed to save himself from the waves and was only waiting to be airlifted off the rocks. Bloody Kenneth and all of his bragging. What a gall it must have been for her to listen when all the while his actions had led to her brother's death.'

The two friends sat together in the conservatory enjoying the cool breeze that came through an open window. The rest of the group had gone upstairs to pack. A dramatic end to their life-support course and one they'd all rather forget. Suzalinna had spoken to Jamie before he had disappeared and promised to arrange some private tuition before he sat his assessment with the next course intake. He seemed genuinely touched by her interest and Cathy thought he'd pass without question, but more importantly, he'd gain some much-needed confidence from it.

'So, what was it Martha did wrong? You said it wasn't

because she saw something in the corridor that night. Why was she looking odd then when Duncan saw her in the lobby?'

'She was down there to talk with Ryan, I believe. They'd been an item years ago. Ryan wanted to pick up where they left off but I doubt Martha had any intention of doing such a thing. Still, though, she agreed to talk to him. She couldn't have him up to the room because I was there, but she said she'd meet him in the lobby. I guess while she was waiting for him she went down the corridor for a nosy,' Cathy said. 'I think she saw the name of the conference room on the door for the first time and well, what a memory. It brought it all back.'

'So, by chance, she had been a locum GP on Skeln when Andrea's brother visited? But why did Andrea hate her so much? It wasn't her fault he died. Surely, she watched in horror like the rest of the islanders? There was nothing she could do other than break the news to the family on the mainland after.'

'You know that expression about shooting the messenger?'

'Oh, come on, Cath, surely there had to be more than that. Andrea stabbed her in the back, quite literally. It was brutal.'

'I don't think Martha did her job particularly well that dreadful day. Maybe it was the first time she had broken bad news to anyone. She'd have just finished her registrar year and was going out into the world as a newly qualified GP. Locuming on Skeln was a bit of an adventure and then that happened. Even I, after many years of practice, wouldn't find the call easy and you know how families latch onto things. I've experienced it myself. They hear one sentence out of ten minutes consolation and it's often a poorly phrased one. I wouldn't be surprised if she mentioned it having been a dangerous place to surf. Maybe it sounded like she was blaming the boy instead of helping them cope with their loss.'

Suzalinna nodded. 'Do you think when Martha arrived here

for the course, she realised that Kenneth had been the helicopter medic involved with the Skeln accident?'

'I doubt it. She wouldn't have seen him, after all, and unless she read up about it later in the papers, how would she know?'

'Well, how did you know, darling?' Suzalinna asked.

'Chris came up with the goods.' She smiled. 'He couldn't sleep properly and managed to do a bit of internet trawling on my behalf. He saw an article about the Skeln residents petitioning for a lifeboat station on the island. The two tragedies were mentioned obviously. One from over forty years ago, the other only five.'

'So, had Andrea planned her revenge? I suppose it was her running away that woke you up that night we discovered poor Martha? You imagined the door handle turning in your anxious state. But for the whole thing to work, there were so many pieces that had to come together for her. We all had to be here...'

'Not really. Just Kenneth. Martha was a bonus and the rest of us didn't matter so much. We were simply pawns in her game. She was very resourceful but she took a foolish risk. She'd done her homework before we all arrived and I think Mr Faber had been a little weak in allowing her such free rein. Even when the hotel's conference suite was refurbished, he took her suggestion on board to name the rooms after islands. A charming idea, Mr Faber thought and so she got her Skeln Suite. She knew that Mr Faber was a kind-hearted man and she played on the fact that he had been involved in an accident himself requiring the help of the emergency services. As things gradually started to fall into place, I doubt she could believe her luck. She had been watching Kenneth's career for some time and knew about the emergency course he was part of. It was hosted by another hotel locally and she realised that if Mr Faber took over, she might finally come into contact with the man that had caused her brother's death.'

'And the nasty letters? What was the purpose of all of that?'

'They had a double purpose. A smokescreen to put us all on the back foot and to make us suspicious of one another but also, she had a real point to make about the medical profession and our lack of integrity. She was right too. Every single one of us had something in our past. Duncan's drinking, your tragic involvement with Roderick, my drug-taking. Then there was poor Jamie. His was the worst. He dearly wanted to redeem himself doing this course but he was greeted by that nasty note.'

'But Ryan didn't get one?'

'I was puzzled by that,' Cathy admitted. 'I suspect it was simply because he had joined the course later on than the rest and so his name wouldn't have been on the list the hotel had of their imminent guests.'

Suzalinna nodded. 'I see. And you said something about the position of Jamie's bed earlier, what did you mean?'

Cathy smiled. 'Well, it gave away who the letter writer was immediately as soon as I heard. Your note was under the bed nearest the door. I assumed that it had been slipped under and you hadn't seen it. Jamie's note though, well, it was by his bed and when I asked him, he mentioned that he slept by the window.'

Suzalinna shook her head. 'I don't get it.'

'Well, it's no wonder Jamie was so paranoid. He was deadly suspicious that his roommate was going to expose his misdemeanour to the rest of us. Ryan was a nasty piece of work actually but Jamie had jumped to the wrong conclusion. He thought Ryan had written and left the note there. It wasn't such a silly idea. It was either Ryan or someone else with a key to the room. Now, admittedly, I managed to nip around the back of reception and get Duncan's room key to look for his note, but would someone chance doing that for all of us? No, as soon as I realised, I knew it had to be a member of the hotel staff and remember too, Andrea was working the night Kenneth died. Perfect opportunity. What could have been easier? She had listened to the resuscitation course lectures all day. She had heard Kenneth blustering and drunkenly boasting over dinner. All that time, she had to serve and pander to him, bringing him whisky after whisky. She must have been incensed.'

Suzalinna sighed. 'How awful. The chief inspector dealt with it very compassionately though. He was glad of your help in the end. You're best chums now, I suppose?'

Cathy blushed and shook her head. 'Hardly that, but at least I've cleared my name, and yours, for that matter. For a while, I thought he was going to arrest us. We did keep stumbling on bodies, didn't we?'

Suzalinna giggled but was serious once more. 'And what about Joan and Charles? Do you think they'll go to Skeln, now? Joan has a bit of a fixation about it, doesn't she? It can't be healthy. And then there was a question about whether that young girl was held under the water and drowned deliberately. It can't be an easy place to return to.'

Cathy had a faraway look in her eyes. She smiled slightly and nodded. 'I think they'll go, yes. And they'll make the best of it. Joan sees it as her duty and I'm sure Charles will ably assist her. Now that the old GP is retiring, the island needs them and it's good to be needed.'

'And what about you, darling? What are you going to do now this is over?'

Cathy smiled fondly at her friend. 'Home to Chris. And I won't be considering anything like this emergency course again. I'm happy to leave the heroics to you and your A&E pals, Suz. Back to the boring GP life for me.'

Suzalinna rolled her eyes. 'Boring? I doubt that. Things seem to happen when you're around. Oh, and one last thing you have still to explain. I know it's a minor point but it was the one thing that I noticed. The light bulb? You said Andrea removed it after killing Kenneth? She must have been in a mad panic though. What did she do with it?'

Cathy smiled and got up. 'I'm not totally sure, but I did have an idea...'

Suzalinna followed her friend into the lobby. 'The police were crawling all over this place and then there was someone on guard practically the whole time so I doubt she'd have had a chance to...'

Cathy reached into the vase in the centre of the circular table. 'Ouch!' she squealed as one of the ornamental thistles jagged her. But undeterred, she tried again. The look of triumph on her face was enough to confirm it even before she withdrew her hand.

'Well, Cathy, you never cease to amaze me,' Suzalinna admitted taking the glass bulb from her friend. 'Perhaps I should write a book about your adventures sometime. 'Dr Cathy Moreland's Mysteries,' I'd call it.'

'Idiot.' Cathy laughed. 'Come on, let's go home. I think I've had quite enough of murder mysteries for now.'

THE END

ACKNOWLEDGEMENTS

Many thanks to the Bloodhound team – especially my brilliant editor Clare. Thanks also to my long-suffering husband and wonderful son for jollying me along and understanding when I have no option but to get the words down! A big thanks go to my dear author friend Caron who has been a massive support since I signed the publishing contract and has made the entire process so much more enjoyable! Finally, thank you to the readers who continue to contact me and tell me that Dr Cathy has meant something to them. When I began writing the series, I had no idea that it would turn into this.

A NOTE FROM THE PUBLISHER

Thank you for reading this book. If you enjoyed it please do consider leaving a review on Amazon to help others find it too.

We hate typos. All of our books have been rigorously edited and proofread, but sometimes mistakes do slip through. If you have spotted a typo, please do let us know and we can get it amended within hours.

info@bloodhoundbooks.com